Half-Penny Sparrows

Cindy McMillion

PublishAmerica
Baltimore

Hardcover 978-1-4512-7538-4
Softcover 978-1-4512-7539-1
PUBLISHED BY PUBLISHAMERICA, LLLP
www.publishamerica.com
Baltimore

Printed in the United States of America

With thanks to Suz, Kim, and Delphia

Are not two sparrows sold for a penny?
Matthew 10:29

Chapter 1

Maybe if I keep my eyes squeezed tight shut, I won't really be here in this strange bed. Maybe I'll still be at home, under my own white chenille spread, listening to the early morning sounds of Mama in the kitchen. Isn't that her I hear now? She's rattling pans and setting the skillet on the stove for frying bacon. That's what Daddy wants first thing, after his coffee. Maybe he's walking down the hall right now, headed for the steaming cup Mama always puts out for him. Maybe he's feeling better this morning and won't be jumping every time Darryl moves. He's little, Daddy, only nine, he doesn't know how bad your nerves are. It'll be ok, just drink your coffee and smell that bacon cooking. Umm-umm. Eggs will be coming along right after, and then the pan of biscuits will be out before you know it. Darryl, come on over and talk to Daddy. Look at him, give him a smile, show him you love him. Don't be sitting over there all sulled up. Who do you think got you that new bike last week? You know he loves you Darryl, and you know he's sorry for hurting you. You should've done what he told you and nothing would have happened, so it's half your own fault anyway. Besides, you're not hurting now, are you? So there. Look here, Mama's got a good breakfast coming. Thank you, Mama. I'll help you carry everything to the table. Darryl, go get Daddy the newspaper. You know he's got to read what all

President Johnson's got to say today about that war over in Vietnam. I don't understand it enough to have my own opinion, but Daddy sure does. He says America ought to get in there and blow every stinking Communist off the face of the earth.

I turn over and hunker down in the bed, trying to find a comfortable spot. Maybe if I could have made Darryl understand, I wouldn't be here now and he wouldn't be God knows where. Maybe we'd be waking up together in the same room, like we did sometimes on those nights when Daddy was sick. It was better to keep real quiet then and maybe even hide in the closet if he started slamming doors too loud. Even if he came in looking for us, he'd forget why he was there in a minute or two, especially if Mama came for him. "Gerald, don't wake the children. Come on to bed now. Come on." And she'd lead him away. Darryl and I would climb back into my bed, but it would take me a long time to get to sleep.

A door opens down the hallway and I hear the sharp tap of high heels on the wooden floor. Gospel music is playing on the TV at the other end of the house, and I know what's coming. I wish I could shut my ears too, not just my eyes.

"Madelyn? Get up and get ready, dear. You know we have to be out of here in an hour." Mrs. Cochran stands in the doorway, not Mama. "I ironed your blue dress and laid it out for you. And don't be wearing those old brown shoes. Margaret Ann has a good pair she can give you. Nothing wrong with them, she's just outgrown them. Get on up." I can hear her heels click away toward Jackie's room next. He's the least one, younger than Darryl and twice as nervous. All you have to do is look at his fingernails. They're chewed clear up into the quick. It's a wonder he doesn't get an infection.

I pull the covers up around me for just another minute. If I thought it would do any good, I would just lie here and make out like I was asleep, but that hasn't worked yet and it's been three weeks already. Two Sundays in all, and now this is the third. We always went to church with Mama back at home, but that was different. We just blended in there. Here, we have to sit on the second row with Mrs. Cochran, while Mr. Cochran preaches. He's the pastor. Everybody's watching us, I know they are, especially me. I try to sit as still and straight as Margaret Ann, who's thirteen, two years older than I am. I don't want to be the subject of anybody's conversation over Sunday dinner. Jackie sits on the other side of his mother and fidgets through the whole thing. He picks his nose sometimes too, which I'm sure drives Mrs. Cochran to distraction. She doesn't seem cut out to be the mother of a boy, in my opinion. I have to agree that nose picking is not an attractive habit, but she's just going to have to get used to some things, like spitting and sweating and smelling bad. Boys can't help that. She's got Jackie so nervous trying to make him perfect that he doesn't know which end's up.

I hear Jackie head toward the bathroom to pee, so I sit up, put my feet on the floor, and look around. The bedroom here is all right, I guess. I can put up with it for no longer than I'm going to be around, although I tell you I'm not in favor of this much pink. The rug, the curtains, even the sheets: all cotton-candy pink. There's some pretty things on the dresser though; a perfume bottle, a silver hairbrush, and a little yellow ceramic bird sitting on a branch, with black eyes and tiny feathers that look almost real. There's my pocket change too, and my lucky penny, but I wouldn't count those. I tried to make my bedroom at home look nice, but I didn't have fancy things to set out everywhere. My best thing was a picture I made myself out of little cut up squares of construction paper, all put together to make a unicorn hiding in the woods. I like to have never got it finished, seeing as how I had to put a dab of glue on the back of each and every little piece before I stuck it on. I know it's what people call a mosaic. Mama gave me a frame, and I hung it on the wall where I could see it every night before I went to sleep.

I get up and dress, all the while wondering what Darryl is doing right now. Is he getting ready for church too? What kind of family is he with? Is somebody doctoring his sore places? You have to be real careful when you put on the ointment or it will sting bad. Also, I hope he's not wetting the bed again. That would definitely not make a good first impression. Somebody needs to remind him not to drink too much in the evening. Maybe I'll ask Ms. Whitten, the social worker, next time she comes, and she'll let me send a letter to his foster parents. They need to know those kinds of things. I don't know why they didn't put us together in the first place.

Breakfast here is quiet, except for the gospel music. Margaret Ann turns it down when Mr. Cochran says the blessing, but then turns if back up a little when he's done. Listening to those quartets gets him in the mood to preach, I guess. If you ask me, those folks on TV are singing with a little more enthusiasm than is necessary for this early in the morning.

Mr. Cochran finishes up his toast and eggs, then pushes back his plate so he can set his big Bible up on the table. I haven't been here long, but I know not to disturb him while he reads over his lesson and finishes his coffee. If I want anything, which I don't, I whisper it to Margaret Ann and she passes it to me. When Mr. Cochran finally shuts the book, it's all right to talk out loud.

"Daddy, what's the sermon about this morning?" Margaret Ann asks as she dabs at her mouth with a napkin and looks at him with those big blue eyes. I don't know how she can do that, look at him straight on, I mean. I know I can't. Mr. Cochran is big and broad-shouldered, with black greased-back hair, and I'd just as soon not have him pay me that much attention. I don't know whether he reminds me more of God because of his shoulders and deep voice or of the devil because of all the yelling he does up there in church. I think I could go either way on this one.

"We're in the book of First Thessalonians," Mr. Cochran replies, clearing his throat as he looks around the table. "Have you children done your Sunday School lessons?" He takes a sip from his second cup of coffee and arches one slick-looking black eyebrow at each one of us in turn. To my way of thinking, there's no call to look so hard at anybody, especially Jackie. He's about to go to pieces.

"Yes sir," we chorus, nodding solemnly.

"Then if you all are finished with breakfast, go get your coats and head on over," Mrs. Cochran orders. "We'll be along in a few minutes."

I follow Margaret Ann down the hall, stopping in the bathroom to brush my teeth. Jackie is right behind me, and I can tell he's trembling even before I turn around.

"Madelyn, I didn't do it," he whispers. I look at him.

"Do what?" I ask.

"My Sunday School page. I didn't do it. I started it, but then I forgot." His eyes are wet and filled with fear. "Daddy'll get on to me."

"It's all right," I whisper back. "I'll help you when we get there."

"But what if Daddy asks to see it before we go? What'll I do?"

I think for a moment. "Go get a pencil," I say. "We can do it right here."

He hurries back with his paper and a little worn out stub.

"Give it to me," I say, "and keep a watch out."

I sit on the edge of the bathtub and fill in all the blanks while Jackie hangs on the door and pokes his head out. It only takes a minute or two. I know the answers because of being at church with Mama all those years.

"Jackie? Madelyn? Come on," we hear Mrs. Cochran say.

I scribble in the last word. "There," I whisper, shoving the paper into Jackie's hand, "nobody'll know the difference."

"We're coming!" I call. I grab our coats from the hall closet on the way out.

We walk from the parsonage down the gravel walkway over to the church. I for one am in no hurry to get there. The air is damp and cold with gray clouds, like it might rain any minute. That's the way November is, and I hate it most of the time.

"Madelyn?" Jackie says, clutching the paper in his sweaty hands. I don't know how he can sweat in the winter, but he does. "Am I going to get in trouble about my lesson?"

"First of all, don't tell anybody," I answer, "Second of all, quit wrinkling it up. If you feel bad, you can ask God to forgive you later. Besides, you meant to finish it, didn't you? That's what counts."

Actually, I think that's what is called "good intentions," which according to Mama pave the way to destruction, but I'll think about that later. Jackie's probably better off facing God than Mr. Cochran anyway. At least he doesn't stare a hole through a person when he asks you something.

We head up the walkway, climb the steps, and go inside. It takes a second to adjust my eyes, even though it's not sunny out, so I stand still and sniff the air. Why is it that churches always smell like furniture polish and carnations? Maybe there's a brand of room spray called *Sunday Morning* that regular people don't know about, that they only sell to pastors. I can tell you right now, I wouldn't buy it.

I am nervous around all these people I don't know, so I finger the lucky penny in my pocket, turning it over and over, taking some comfort in the feel of it. It's not a penny exactly, it's a coin from Germany that my Uncle Jimmy gave me when I was six, and I always carry it with me. I don't know if it does any good or not, but it sure doesn't do any harm. I'm just glad I had it with me the day we got taken away.

Margaret Ann is waiting for us in the vestibule, standing over by the water fountain. I wish I was tall and pretty like her and had that curly blonde hair. She knows just how to smile and talk to the ladies in their fancy dresses. I wonder if she ever does anything wrong. So far, I haven't seen any evidence of it, although I know for a fact that appearances don't always tell you everything about a person. Sometimes the bad parts are hidden down deep, and it takes a while for them to come out.

Take Daddy for instance. Most people would say, "What a hard worker. He takes such good care of his family." And they'd be right about that part. But they might be surprised to learn about some of his less attractive features. For one thing, he never can seem to let up on Darryl. Lord knows Darryl tried to please him, but he never could quite do it. He was always spilling something or dropping something or breaking something. He never was too good at schoolwork either, which also got on Daddy's nerves. Daddy would look over Darryl's shoulder when he was doing homework at the kitchen table and say, "What's this mess?" and then start telling him how to do it right. He meant well by trying to teach his own son, but Darryl just couldn't seem to get the multiplication tables straight in his head. Daddy's voice would get louder and louder as Darryl wrote and erased and wrote again.

"Are you stupid, son? Is that it?" Daddy would finally holler, "or are you just not paying attention? Now get this right or you'll wish you had!" Darryl would be shaking by then and have his paper erased clear through in spots. Still, the answers would be wrong.

And that's when Daddy's belt would come off, with that terrible swishing sound as he yanked it through the loops. He would jerk Darryl up by his arm and whip him over and over across his back and legs. Darryl would be jumping around and screaming and begging him, "No, no, Daddy, please no! Daddy, no! I love you! I love you!" and finally it would be over. Darryl would collapse in a wet heap on the floor, and Daddy would leave out, slamming the door behind him.

I used to wonder why Mama didn't stop him, but I don't guess she could have even if she had tried. Daddy was too big and too strong. She would be standing at the kitchen sink washing dishes and wouldn't even turn around the whole time. I looked over at her once during one of those whippings and saw that she was washing the same blue cup over and over and just staring down into the soapsuds. Every time after Daddy left, she would come over and help Darryl up and sit him in a chair. Sometimes I wanted to scream at her because she just stood there and let Daddy do what he did, but I never said anything. I didn't figure I ought to be ordering my own Mama around.

"Your daddy loves you," she'd tell Darryl, pulling up a chair for herself and wiping his tears with a wadded up tissue from her pocket. After he had calmed down some, she'd say, "He never had a chance to finish school, you know, and he wants you to have a better life than he had. He doesn't want you to have to work in the factory when you're grown. He wants you to make good grades so you can go on to college and be whatever you want to be. Now go wash your face and come back in here and finish this homework. He loves you, Darryl; he just wants what's best for you." Then she'd tuck her hair behind her ear, get up, and go back to washing dishes, and I'd sit by Darryl and whisper him the answers. If I'd been thinking, I'd have done that in the first place and we'd have been spared the whole thing, but I didn't.

I never told anybody about Daddy, but Darryl was of a different mind, and after a while he just got fed up. I blame his teacher, mostly. She kept nosing into our business, asking him where did he get that mark on his arm or what happened to his cheek. He always mumbled out something, but she wouldn't quit pestering him. I told Darryl not to let on about anything that went on at home, as I had heard about kids being taken away from their parents, but he wouldn't listen to me.

It all came to a head one night in October.

That night Daddy came in late, and I could hear him stomping down the hall toward Darryl's room. We had already been asleep two or three hours, but I could see Darryl's light come on and Daddy commenced to hollering and pushing furniture around. Then came the screaming and the whipping and the crying. Darryl was shrieking, "I'm sorry, Daddy! I'm sorry! I'm sorry! I'll do it!" The belt was smacking hard, over and over, for what seemed like forever, and I hated Daddy like I've never hated anybody in my life. If I'd had a gun, I would have shot him right through the heart, I promise I would have. Then, finally, it stopped and I heard heavy footsteps go past my door. I waited for a minute, then slipped out to Darryl's room. He was just lying there on top of the covers, sobbing, and I lay down beside him. It was too dark to see anything, but I put one arm across him and he flinched, so I drew back. I didn't know exactly where he'd been hit and I didn't want to hurt him more. So I just lay there and tried to hold his hand, but he jerked away.

"I hate him, I hate him, I hate him!" he gasped between his crying. "I hate him!"

I moved in closer. "I do too," I whispered back.

"I'm going to kill him!" he choked out.

Now, that shocked me, even though I was thinking the very same thing not five minutes earlier. But I could hear something in

Darryl's voice that hadn't ever been there before, and it made my hair stand on end.

"What did you do to make him so mad?" I asked.

"He said I didn't take out the trash."

"Did you?"

"I forgot."

His words were muffled into the pillow, and I didn't know what to answer, so I just lay there a while longer, listening to him cry until he finally cried himself to sleep. Then I got up very quietly and headed back to my room. I stopped by the bathroom to get a drink of water and turned on bathroom light. That's when I saw it. The whole side of my pajamas where I had lain up against Darryl was streaked with blood. God Almighty, what had Daddy done to him? He'd beaten him like a dog, that's what, beaten his own son. God, I wanted to kill him all over again.

I started to go wash the blood off Darryl, but I didn't want to wake him up, so I just changed my pajamas, got a blanket, and went back to Darryl's room. Then I felt around in the closet for his baseball bat and put it down beside me. If Daddy came back, I'd be ready.

The next morning at breakfast Darryl didn't say much. Mama cooked pancakes and bacon, Darryl's favorite, and we ate, then went on down to the bus stop. Darryl was stiff when he walked and didn't go very fast. We climbed on the bus and I sat with my friend Angela. Darryl sat by himself a few seats up. He just looked out the window the whole time and didn't speak to anybody. I could see his reflection from where I was, and it seemed like he was staring at something far away.

At nine-thirty that morning, Miss Clayton, the school counselor, knocked on my classroom door and called Mrs. Greer out in the hallway. We were all working on an adjective page, I remember, and everybody was quiet. We could hear them talking outside the door, but only the murmur, not the words. Then Mrs. Greer stepped back in and called softly, "Madelyn, get your things please and come with me." I almost forgot my coat, but she sent me back for it, and I followed her out. She sent me on with Miss Clayton toward the office.

"What's wrong?" I asked. "Am I checking out? Is somebody sick?"

"Madelyn," Miss Clayton answered, stopping to look at me in the face, "do you know about your brother getting hurt?"

"What do you mean?" I asked, my heart suddenly flipping over, icy cold in my chest.

"He's covered with belt marks," she said. "Do you know who did this?"

"I-I don't know what you're talking about," I finally stammered. My whole body was shaking by then. The hall was hollow and echoing, and something was sucking the air straight out of my lungs. I didn't try to say anything else.

Miss Clayton stared straight at me for a long moment before she spoke again. I could tell she wasn't quite sure how to say what she had on her mind. So we started walking again, my knees wobbling, and she finally found her tongue.

"Madelyn, I have to tell you that the police and a social worker are in the nurse's office. You're going to have to talk to them. I know this is scary, but honey, it's very important that you tell them what happened to your brother and answer any questions they have."

"How did they...?"

"Darryl told his teacher this morning. He did the right thing, Madelyn. No matter how bad it seems right now, he did exactly the right thing by telling. The nurse is with him now, cleaning him up and helping him." We were in front of the door by then. "Now come on in with me." She turned the knob, and we stepped inside.

"Madelyn? Madelyn?" I am back in the church vestibule and Jackie is tugging at my sleeve. I look down, almost startled to see his face rather than Darryl's. "Can you walk me to my Sunday School class?" He is already pulling me down the hall, so I drop him off with his teacher and head slowly on toward my own class.

Going to Sunday School is not on my list of favorite things, but it looks to me like I'm fresh out of choices. My lucky penny is warm in the pocket of my coat. It reminds me that I won't be here long, and that I can stand anything for a little while.

Chapter 2

The only thing I really like about church is the singing. Some of my favorite songs are hymns, I don't mind saying. They always make Jesus sound like somebody you'd like to sit by at lunch. He seems kind, and like he'd listen if you wanted to tell him your secrets. I especially like *Softly and Tenderly Jesus is Calling*. I could hear that one every week and never get tired of it. When we sing about him standing on the portals waiting and watching, I get a good, warm feeling inside, like he's glad to see me. If church was nothing but singing, I could get along all right, but they always have to throw in the preaching. The way I see it, it ruins the mood.

Take now for instance. Mr. Cochran is sweating up a storm there in the pulpit. Why he's so intent on shouting, I don't know. We're not but fifteen feet away from him, if that. He might be dressed up nice, but it would help his looks one hundred percent if he would calm down and smile once in a while. That's my opinion, which nobody asked for, but which I have anyway. Beside me, Margaret Ann is holding the Holy Bible and turning to the parts he mentions. I might do the same, but I didn't think to bring mine when we left the house this morning. I was in too big a hurry. On the other side of Mrs. Cochran, Jackie starts swinging his legs and kicking the seat in front of him, but his mama puts a stop to that in a red-hot minute.

This has been going on for nearly an hour, according to my watch, and ought to be winding down any time now. My bottom gets sore from sitting so long, not to mention the difficulty of keeping my mind on the business at hand.

Mr. Cochran pauses to wipe his brow with one of the fresh white handkerchiefs Margaret Ann ironed yesterday. She even irons his shorts, which I consider extreme, since nobody sees them anyway. But to each his own.

"I'm here to tell you, friends," he bellows, "God knows every thought of your heart, every word you speak, every deed you do. There's a great day coming, when every one of us will stand before the throne of God and give an account to Him. Are you ready, brothers? Are you ready, sisters?" He grips the sides of the pulpit and gazes out over the audience, eyes burning.

I don't turn around, but I can feel some uncomfortable shifting behind me, which could mean one of two things: either somebody besides me is ready for this to end, or there's a guilty sinner examining his conscience.

We stand and sing, with Mr. Cochran up there at the front, waiting to see if he can flush anybody out, but nobody comes, so we sit back down and get ready to pray and hand over our money.

Speaking of guilty sinners, I wonder what God thinks of Darryl and me wanting to kill Daddy that night. From what Mr. Cochran says, Daddy shouldn't be treating his family so mean, but I'm thinking he wouldn't look on the two of us committing murder too kindly either. Either way, he's watching us and knows what we're thinking. I don't understand how he has time to spend sifting through the thoughts and words of every single person on earth. One thing that must make his job easier is that there is daylight on only one side of the world at a time, so the people on the other side are asleep. That way he only has to deal with half the

20

people at a time. Even so, that's a lot. I'm glad I'm not him. Just thinking about it makes me tired.

Another thing I don't understand is why he wasn't listening all those times I asked him to make Daddy stop hurting Darryl. I would think that anybody who created the world could do something about that. He could have toned Daddy down some and made him see things in a different light. Seems to me it wouldn't be any more trouble to him than flicking a fly.

I know Daddy has a lot of good in him, so I guess I wouldn't really want to kill him, even if he is mean as a snake sometimes. He showed me how to tie my shoes when I was five, and he always smiled and gave me money when I brought home a good report card, which I did on a routine basis. He was good to Darryl a lot of times too, letting him work on the car with him on Saturday mornings, calling him his little buddy, and taking him along when he had to buy parts at the hardware store. Darryl walked just like him, with that little bit of a swagger. They are both dark-headed and watched sports together on TV. Darryl would prop his legs up on the coffee table just like Daddy, and they'd eat popcorn and yell for their favorite teams.

When he was being nice, it was hard to imagine he could get so all-fired mad. We'd be going along just fine, but then the bills would start piling up or something around the house wouldn't get done to his satisfaction. Sometimes it was Mama he yelled at, but mostly it was Darryl. He didn't hardly ever yell at me because I always jumped to do whatever he said and more. I tried to make Darryl do the same, but he gets distracted easy. Maybe if we had both tried a little harder, everything would have been ok. Whenever we get back home, I'm going to sit down with Darryl and make him write out a list of what he's supposed to do and not do and make sure he follows it. Then Daddy will be pleased and proud of his good family.

We all stand for the closing prayer and church is finally over until this evening, when we'll have to come back and do it all over again. That's the trouble with living in a pastor's house. You have to go to church every time, even when you really wish you could stay home and watch something good on TV. We step out of the pew, and I mill around with Jackie until Mrs. Cochran is ready to leave. I wouldn't mind talking to someone my own age, but nobody comes up. I see a girl I recognize from school, Lindsey Sutton, talking to some other girls, but I don't know her well enough to go up and join in. Besides, I don't know if she would want to be friends with me. Maybe I can try talking to her tomorrow at recess.

We leave church, have a big dinner of roast beef, potatoes, and carrots, then clean up and have the afternoon to ourselves. I knock on Margaret Ann's bedroom door and she says to come in. I don't know what I thought a foster sister would be like, but I have to say this one is sweet and kind. She has pretty yellow comforters on her twin beds, and she invites me to turn the covers back and lie down on one of them. She's got a book and tells me I can pick one off her shelf to read. I get one about a horse that looks good, and I stack some pillows so I can lean back. It feels friendlier than it does in my room, and I wish I could stay in here tonight. I know nobody is going to bother me, but I don't like sleeping alone in a house where I don't belong. The horse story turns out to be interesting, about a boy who rescues an injured wild stallion and tames it. We read quietly for a while, then Margaret Ann yawns and closes her book.

"Want to take a nap?" she asks. I don't, but not wanting to be thought of as uncooperative, I say yes and lay my book on the night table. She closes her eyes and scoots down a little in the bed. I never took naps at home. There was always something on TV or some work to do around the house. If I didn't have anything else to do, I liked organizing my room and deciding where to put everything. Socks and underwear in the top drawer, pajamas and tee shirts in the next drawer down, then sweaters on the bottom. Shirts and dresses and pants I hung in the closet, and I lined my shoes up on the closet floor. I even had hooks on the inside closet wall where I hung necklaces that would otherwise get tangled up in my jewelry box. Then I'd stack games on the shelf and put away most of the stuff on my dresser, like hair barrettes and my comb. I liked doing Darryl's room too. He threw things every which a way, and it was satisfying to see it looking all straight and nice when I finished.

"Madelyn?" Margaret Ann says, startling me. I thought she was asleep, but she isn't. In fact, she's turned on her side now and is propped on her elbow looking at me.

"What?" I lean on my elbow too and face her.

"I hope you don't mind me asking," she says with some hesitation, "but what is your family like? I mean, do you have any brothers or sisters?"

"Yes," I answer, "I have a brother. And a mama and daddy." I can tell she wants to know more, but I don't want to say anything I might wish later I'd kept my mouth shut about.

"I'm glad you're here," she says. "Last year we had two other foster children. One was a baby, and the other one was four years old."

"What happened to them?" I ask.

"They stayed for about eight months, then they went back to their family. Their mother was in jail for something and didn't have anybody to keep them. I don't think they had a father. So they came here." She twirls the end of her hair. "I miss them, especially the baby. She was so sweet. I used to bathe her and dress her up in these cute little dresses and play with her."

"What about the other one?"

"He was a boy and was all right too. Mostly Jackie played with him."

"Do you ever see them anymore?" I ask.

"No. Once they leave, they're just gone. It's always like that. We've kept eleven foster kids in all, including you. Sometimes I think I could just die when they leave." She pauses. "I worry about them all the time. You know, wondering if they're ok. Some of them get adopted and I think they're all right, but most of them go back to the family they came from. It scares me to think about that. I mean, you hope their parents are treating them right, but you never know."

I look at her without saying anything for a minute.

"In case you're wondering, my parents treat my brother and me fine," I say. "They just have some money problems right now. My daddy hurt his back on the job and had to be in the hospital for three months, so we were running low on funds, you know. It's going to take Daddy a while to get well. He has to stay in the bed all the time, so Mama's going back to work. We're just here till he gets back on his feet."

"Oh," Margaret Ann says, "that's good."

"Yeah," I answer, "so you don't have to worry about us. This is purely financial. My daddy earned a lot of money, so naturally this is hard on him. He'll be all right though. He's a good worker."

I am shocked at how easily that story slides out of my mouth. I didn't know I was such a good liar, but I must be because Margaret Ann looks relieved that I have such a fine family to go back to.

"What's your mama like?" she asks, more relaxed now.

"Oh, Mama," I laugh, "she's a lot of fun. She's good at sports too. Last summer the ladies softball team she's on won the league championship. She was the pitcher."

"Really?" says Margaret Ann. "I can't imagine my mama doing something like that." We both giggle at the thought of Mrs. Cochran speeding around the bases in her dress and high heels.

"Mama's the room mother at my old school too," I say. "She organizes the refreshments at Christmas and Easter. Also, she likes to throw dinner parties at home." I roll my eyes and grin. "You know, all that fancy china and silver. She has a party about every week."

Margaret Ann is impressed, I can tell. I just hope Mr. Cochran was wrong about God hearing everything we say. If he's listening to this, his mouth is hanging open, and he's probably looking down here to make sure this is really me, Madelyn, he's hearing.

"Well," says Margaret Ann, smiling, "that's good." She rolls back over on her back and shuts her eyes again. I'm glad she's done asking questions. No telling what else Mama would have accomplished if I'd kept talking. I turn over and pull the comforter up under my chin.

What is Mama doing now? I wonder. And Daddy. What about Daddy? I hope those policemen gave him a good talking-to. I know that would help. They could make him understand that no sir, he is not to whip his children that a way. He's doing it too hard, even if he is just trying to teach Darryl a lesson and make him do right. Losing his children for a few weeks must have shocked him for sure. I know he never thought anything like that could happen. Daddy's never been in trouble with the police before. I wonder what the neighbors were thinking when they saw patrol cars in our driveway.

Daddy's probably got a big apology all ready for Darryl. Maybe he even wrote it down to show the police so they will know how sorry he is. Our family will be all right after this. I just know it. Daddy understands what's expected of him now.

I scoot around to get more comfortable, trying to be quiet so as not to wake Margaret Ann. Evidently, nobody does anything around here on Sundays but read and take naps. I don't even hear Jackie in the house. Except for the clock ticking on the night table, it's quiet and still, which leaves me with too much time on my hands. Maybe if I'd had a little more of that back at home, I'd have come up with a way of working things out.

Finally, I can't keep still any longer, so I slip out of bed and go back to my room. I call it mine, although according to Margaret Ann, I'm not the only one who has lived in here. I take out a plain white piece of paper, a pencil, and some markers. This will be a good chance to make a card for Lindsey, that girl I want to talk to tomorrow. I fold the paper carefully in half, then in half again, and draw a border of blue and purple flowers on the front, connected with a green vine. Next I have to think of what to say. Finally I settle on a fancy *Hello* on the outside and a note on the inside that says, *Would you like to sit with me at lunch tomorrow? Your friend, Madelyn.* I add a few stray flowers to the inside and then stick it inside my Bible so it won't get wrinkled up before I can get it to her tonight. Neatness counts when you're trying to make a good impression.

Then I take out another sheet to make a card for Mama. Ms. Whitten, the social worker, is coming for a visit on Tuesday, and she can give it to Mama, except I don't know what to say. This will be my first ever letter to write to her, not counting the one I did in third grade to practice penmanship. What do you write to your own mama? *I hope you are doing all right?* No, that sounds like something to say to a stranger. *What have you been up to lately?* No, not that either; it sounds like she's been too busy to think about me, and I know that's not the case. I decide to decorate first and write later. But even after I have the yellow rose border all around, my mind is still as blank as the inside of the card.

Finally, I get out a regular sheet of paper so I can practice what I want to say before I mess up trying to figure out how to put it.

> *Dear Mama,*
> *This is Madelyn. Surprise, surprise! I bet you weren't expecting to get a letter from me. I am fine. I don't know if Darryl is fine or not, as I haven't seen him. I am staying with a preacher's family and they are very nice. I miss you and Daddy. Tell Daddy I love him and Darryl loves him and he is sorry for not taking out the trash or doing his homework right. Tell Daddy it's all right that he got a little over-angry. I know he didn't mean to. Everybody gets mad sometimes. How are you, Mama? Ms. Whitten says we will see you on Thursday. Goodbye for now.*
> *Sincerely, Madelyn*

There's a soft knock on my door and Margaret Ann is standing there, waiting for me to walk back to church with her, so I don't get to copy it over, but I will later. Jackie stays home with Mrs. Cochran because he's taking a cold, so I grab my Bible and we head out.

Right off, I notice Lindsey in the vestibule with her mother and some other grownups. I take a deep breath and decide to speak to her as we pass and hand her the card I made, but when I say hello, she just looks at me with a nasty little smirk on her face and says, "Aren't you the new foster child?" I stand there with my mouth halfway open, too shocked to answer back. When her mother's done talking, they both turn and walk off toward the sanctuary. Lindsay twists her head around and smirks at me again, and for a minute, I don't even move. She's the first person outside Mr. Franklin, the art teacher, that I've gotten up the nerve to talk to at church or school, and all she can say is "Aren't you the foster child?"

I walk back over to Margaret Ann and we go sit down on the second row, but I don't hear anything that goes on. I stand when I'm supposed to stand and sit when I'm supposed to sit, but in my mind I'm floating somewhere up by the ceiling, looking down, with all the words and songs coming to me from far away. Is that what everyone thinks of me now? That I'm just some foster child the Cochrans took in? Don't they even care if I have a name or not? My face is burning, and I feel too ashamed to look at anybody.

My hands are in my lap, but they don't even seem like mine anymore. They belong to a stranger. I can't take a good breath, and my mouth is dried out. All I can think of is what a mess I'm in, a charity case living with some family I don't even know. Why can't I go home? Why did Darryl have to tell? We could have talked some sense into Daddy. We could have told him that we'd be good from then on and that he wouldn't have to worry himself about us ever again. I want to go home and be in my own house, in my own school and with my own friends. I want to be who I was before.

Church is finally over. Margaret Ann stands up and I do too, but slowly, because I'm not sure my legs will hold me. Then I look over and see Lindsey across the sanctuary with her turned-up nose and fake fur jacket, and something hard and fearless wakes up inside of me. Before I know it, I'm walking toward her. I don't see anyone else along the way. I take a short breath and then a longer one. One foot in front of the other is all I have to do. I've got a thing or two to tell that little stuck-up priss, and I aim to tell it. She may think she can make me a nobody, but she can't. She can't. I'm Madelyn Bradshaw. I have a name. I make good grades and I'm good at art and I even know how to make blackberry cobbler from scratch. I bet Lindsay can't do any of that. She's not the queen of the world, and I don't have to listen to her. Just because she said something doesn't make it true. I'd like to slap her stupid face. The closer I get, the better I can breathe. I don't know why I ever thought I wanted to be friends with her in the first place. She sees me coming and gets that smart aleck look on her face again, but it changes when I'm still a good ten feet away. That's when her eyes get big and she looks around like she's ready to shout for help.

I stand looking right at her for a minute, then say straight out, but soft so that nobody else can hear me, "In case you want to know, you little pig, my name is Madelyn."

I turn and walk out of the sanctuary, not waiting for anybody. As soon as I hit the front door, I start running up the hill through the wet leaves to the parsonage, and I don't stop till I get to my own room. I shake my Bible upside down and the card with the blue and purple flowers falls out. I stomp on it with my dirty shoes, grind it into the floor, and then rip it into a million pieces.

I grab Mama's card off the dresser and lie flat down on the floor on my stomach. I take my pencil and write hard, so hard that I stab the paper in five places.

> *Mama,*
> *Why didn't you stop him ever? Why didn't you call the police? You're the grownup! You could have done something! Why did you let him hurt Darryl over and over again? Why didn't you leave him? You saw what he did and you didn't leave him! It's your fault I'm here in this stupid place! I hate everybody here and everybody hates me!*
> *Sincerely, Madelyn*

Chapter 3

If I thought it was hard being the new girl at school before, boy oh boy, it's ten times worse now. That Lindsay has told the whole sixth grade that I called her a name, and now none of the girls will even look at me. She conveniently left out the fact that she herself acted like a spoiled brat, but I don't care. I just keep my head down and do my work, which I must say I'm very good at. Math has always been my best subject. It's satisfying to line the problems up and work them out and not have to wonder if somebody's going to like the answers or not. English is not like that. When Mrs. Abernathy assigns us something to write about, there's no telling what she wants. To be on the safe side, I generally try to work a dog or cat into my stories because most people like pets.

Today, though, she's having us write about ourselves, especially how we do or do not look like other people in our family. She says it has something to do with us studying genes in science and how blonde-headed parents most generally have blonde-headed children and so forth. I know for a fact that if I was adopted, like my friend Angela at my old school, I would say who I looked like was nobody's business. Besides, I think it might be cheating to mix science and English, although she didn't ask my opinion.

I get out a fresh sheet of paper and write my name at the top. I don't know what the Cochrans told the school about me, but Mrs. Abernathy treats me the same as everybody else, so maybe she hasn't gotten the word yet.

I sharpen up my pencil and start.

> *My name is Madelyn Bradshaw and I'm eleven.*
> *Everybody says I take after my Daddy, who is a good-looking man and very nice. I have his brown eyes, and my hair is dark brown and wavy like his, only mine is long, whereas he is getting bald on top. In my other features, I take after Mama, although my legs are skinnier than hers. Mama has curly brown hair, green eyes, and dimples. I don't have any brothers or sisters, so I wouldn't know whether I look like them or not. Right now I am staying with my aunt and uncle, Robert and Lorraine Cochran, because my parents are traveling in Europe. I look like the Cochrans too, except for their daughter Margaret Ann, who is blonde. She is my cousin and is a very nice person.*

After a while, Mrs. Abernathy takes up the papers and then does something she has never done before. She puts a chart up on the board, labels it for eye color and hair color, and makes an announcement.

"Class, I am going to read your papers out loud and when I get to yours, come up and draw an X in the appropriate boxes on the chart. That way we can see how many of you got your parents' dominant genes and how many got the recessive ones." She leans back against the front of her desk, puts on her reading glasses, and picks up the first composition. "Randall Smithy," she says and looks up. Randall grins. He wouldn't care if he came from a family of kangaroos. All he cares about is getting a laugh.

I am Randall Smithy the Third, Esquire, Mrs. Abernathy reads. *I have the most beautiful parents in the world. That's why I'm so handsome. My two sisters look like they came from Jupiter. They are both stupider. One of them has huge buckteeth and a nose as big as a doorknob. The other one's got four chins and her hair sticks straight out.*

The class is cracking up, the boys most of all. Mrs. Abernathy has a few words to say to Randall, but I don't hear any of it. All I can hear is the blood pounding in my ears. I swallow a few times, thinking Lord, oh Lord, what am I going to do now? Mrs. Abernathy picks up another paper and begins to read. It turns out to be Laura's. Next is Kenny's, then Michael's and Katie's and Sarah's and Wilma's. God, please don't let her read mine, I pray, please, please, please. By the time she starts on Jenna's, the end of my shirt is twisted into a wet knot. God, I promise I will do anything you say for the rest of my life if you will just make the teacher skip mine. God, God, God, please. Mrs. Abernathy picks up another paper.

My name is Madelyn Bradshaw, she begins, *and I'm eleven. Everybody says I take after my Daddy, who is a good-looking man and very nice. I have his brown eyes…*

I am frozen, staring at her, hearing every word loud and clear, until she gets near the end. *Right now I am staying with my aunt and uncle, Robert and Lorraine Cochran, because my parents are traveling in—* she stops and clears her throat. About that time I hear somebody laugh, then two or three giggles from girls behind me. My cheeks are blazing hot, and I put my head down on the desk and pull my coat up over it.

"Boys and girls!" the teacher says sharply, and the laughing stops, but it's too late. I can feel every eye on me, even with my head covered. Nobody says anything for a long minute. Then I hear, "Annie, yours is next. Come up to the board please." She reads the rest of the compositions and I guess everybody marks their hair color in the boxes. I don't know, though, because I've seen all I plan on seeing today. It's safe and dark here, and Miss Madelyn is not coming out.

It wasn't like this at my old school. I rode the bus every day and liked my teacher and had friends and did my work and everything was just normal. If Darryl had kept his big mouth shut, I wouldn't even be here. I'd be sitting with Marian and Angela back at Oak Valley Elementary, minding my own business. Now here I am on the other side of the county and feeling like a sack of garbage somebody has tossed out on the side of the road.

As soon as I can breathe regular again, I look for a spot of light coming in under my coat so I can get some fresh air. I hear Mrs. Abernathy tell the class to get out their social studies books and answer the questions on page 118, but I don't care. After a while, she walks past my desk and puts her hand on my shoulder, but I jerk away, so she moves on. I don't need anybody, teacher or otherwise, feeling sorry for me.

Everybody finishes the lesson and then does spelling. I know it's getting close to lunchtime because my stomach is growling. Sure enough, Mrs. Abernathy lines everybody up and they head to the cafeteria. My desk is by the door, so she leans over and asks if I am hungry, but I don't answer. She probably thinks I'm asleep, so she goes on out.

As soon as the door closes, I throw my coat off and sit up. I don't know what to do next, but I know I'm not staying in here. First thing, I have to go to the bathroom. I get my books and peek out the door, but I don't see my class, so I grab the hall pass and go. That pass will buy me some time and keep people from asking me where I'm going and what I'm up to.

After I use the bathroom, I wash my face and look in the mirror. It almost looks like a stranger staring back at me. My hair's all messed up and I've got dark places under my eyes. Plus, I'm wearing some of Margaret Ann's old clothes she outgrew. When the social workers took Darryl and me that day, I didn't have a chance to go back home and get any of my own. All I brought was what I was wearing. This turquoise sweater is definitely not something I would have picked out, but it's not polite to be so particular.

I finish up in the bathroom, but I don't know where I'm going at first. Lunch is only thirty minutes, so I know I don't have much time to make a plan. Then I remember Mr. Franklin, who teaches art down on the first floor. Our class goes there every Friday afternoon, so I've only been to his room three times, but I like him. He is old, probably about forty, but he never yells at anybody, even if they spill something. His door is open and I look in, but I don't see any kids, only him, setting paints and brushes out on the tables, and I can hear soft music playing. He turns toward me with a friendly smile when I knock.

"I'm Madelyn Bradshaw," I say in a rush because I'm nervous. I've only spoken to him once before and that was to say thank you when he told me he liked the charcoal picture of a face I did last week. "I'm in Mrs. Abernathy's sixth grade. Do you remember me?"

His eyes crinkle at the corners. "Of course, Madelyn, come on in. What do you need, dear?" He stands there like he's waiting for me to give him a note.

I look around, trying to decide what to say. I could make up something about how my teacher sent me down here, but I'm just too upset to think of a good story. In fact, I don't say anything for about a minute, but finally I blurt out, "Mr. Franklin, I need somewhere to stay for the rest of the day. I'm not going back to my class."

He looks surprised and concerned, but he says, "I'll need to check with your teacher, but you're welcome to stay if it's all right with her." While he's gone, I look for a spot where I won't be in the way. There's a table off to one side where he keeps coffee cans full of markers and pens, so I push some of the cans back to make room for my books and sit down.

Mr. Franklin is back in a few minutes with a list of assignments from Mrs. Abernathy. He walks over and sets the paper by the cans. "Your teacher says you've had a pretty rough morning, Madelyn," he says gently as he pulls out a chair and sits down across from me. I look at him without saying a word. "It's hard on anyone starting a new school, and I would think it would be especially difficult under these circumstances."

"Do you know what happened?" I ask.

He nods. "Your teacher told me."

I can taste blood where I'm biting my lip. "Does everybody know I'm a foster child?" I ask.

"This is a small town, Madelyn," he answers, "and the Cochrans have kept a lot of children over the years."

"I'm just staying for a little while," I say. "I have a home. My father got hurt on the job, and we ran out of money trying to pay the hospital. I'll be leaving soon."

He nods again and is quiet. All I can hear is the soft music, with no words, playing in the background. It's like the music I used to turn on to try to get to sleep on those nights when Daddy was sick, and I brought Darryl into my bed.

"Mrs. Abernathy feels badly about the assignment she gave," he said. "She said she just wasn't thinking when she decided to read them aloud. Teachers make mistakes like everybody else, unfortunately."

"Do I have to go back to my class tomorrow?" I ask.

"Yes," he says, "you do."

"But I can come here if I need to?" I ask.

"Yes," he answers, "you can always come here, but I want you to understand something."

I stiffen up. Here it comes, I think. He's going to give me a lecture about how if he lets me run down here anytime I want to, then he'll have to let everybody run down here and what kind of school would that be, so I'd better straighten up and do what I'm told and stay where I'm supposed to.

Mr. Franklin leans forward and props his elbows on his knees. I notice he has paint on his hands and under his fingernails, not to mention all over his clothes. Teaching art is a messy job.

"There is one thing I want you to understand," he says, looking straight at me with kind eyes. "You are a person, Madelyn, and that makes you just as important and valuable as any other person in this school or this town or this world. I know this is a tough time for you, but that doesn't change who you are or what you're worth, no matter what anyone says."

I must look like I don't believe him because he glances around the room for a minute and then gets up and brings two vases back to the table. One is tall and blue, with streaks of gold in it. It is smooth all over, and would look right at home in a rich person's living room. The other one is nothing special, just short and square with a big opening at the top.

"I really enjoy making pottery," he says, turning the blue vase over in his hands. "It's rewarding to me to take clay and work it until it's just right, then turn it into something beautiful or useful." He sets that one down and picks up the short one. "I made both of these a couple of years ago. Can you guess which one I like best?"

I don't have to think about it. I know a trick question when I hear one. He wants me to say the blue one, but I don't. "You like the square one better," I say.

He smiles, "Nope. I made them both, remember? They look different, and I made them for different purposes, that's all. This one," he says, holding the blue one, "is made to hold flowers. And this one," he picks up the short one, "is where I put my pocket change. When it's full, I dump it out and go buy myself some ice cream." His eyes crinkle, and I find myself smiling back for the first time today.

There is a knock at the door, and he hops up. "Second grade is here," he says, leading all the little kids in. "Better get busy on that work Mrs. Abernathy sent down for you." I take out my book and start on social studies page 118.

* * *

It's not until I see her car in the driveway that I remember that the social worker is coming this afternoon. Ms. Whitten is sitting at the kitchen table having a cup of coffee with Mrs. Cochran. I just hope the school hasn't called either one of them. They both look up when I come in and nobody looks mad, so I guess I'm safe for now. I put my coat and books down in a chair.

"Hello, Madelyn," says Ms. Whitten, "how are you?" She's wearing a business suit and has her hair pulled back in a clip. She also has papers from her black briefcase spread out on the table.

"I'm fine," I answer. Nobody says anything about me sitting down, so I don't.

"I'm glad to hear that," she says. "Mrs. Cochran says you are doing very well here and that you seem to be adjusting to school and making good grades."

"Yes ma'am," I say.

"That's wonderful. Your school records indicate that you've always been a good student."

"Yes ma'am."

"Do you like your new foster family?" she asks.

Even if I didn't, I wouldn't be saying so in front of Mrs. Cochran, so naturally I answer yes. I wonder if social workers have a list of questions they're supposed to ask and check off. Maybe that's what some of those papers are for. But I have a few questions of my own.

"Where is Darryl?" I ask.

Ms. Whitten takes off her glasses and motions me to a chair. "Darryl is fine," she says. "He's with a good family and is doing very well. You'll get to see him on Thursday when I take you all for a visit with your mother."

"When am I going home?" I ask. "I'm ready right now. I can go get my stuff."

Ms. Whitten sighs and puts down the folder she's holding. "Madelyn, I know this is difficult for you. It's always hard on children and parents when they have to be separated. Your mother is fine, but she understands that some things have to change before you can return. The courts want to be assured that it will be a safe place for you and your brother."

"It will be safe," I say. "I know what to do if Daddy gets mad at Darryl again. But he won't. I know he won't. The police talked to him, and I know he's going to do better."

"I understand," Ms. Whitten answers, "but both parents are responsible when a child is mistreated. The parent who allows it to go on and doesn't call the authorities is just as liable. Your father was charged but is out on bail and still living in the home. They both have to fulfill the requirements of the court before you can return."

"What do you mean? What do they have to do?"

"Both of them have to complete parent training classes and agree to have a monitor check in on them on a monthly basis for the next two years. Also, your father has to be clean and sober for six months."

"Six months?" I say, maybe too loudly but I don't care. "I thought we were just going to be here for a few weeks. I thought we were going home."

"Six months minimum," answers Ms. Whitten. "That is, if both parents comply with the orders. There's going to be a hearing soon."

"Will Daddy go to jail?" I ask.

"That will depend on the judge. If your father attends the parenting classes and AA meetings, he may not have to serve time. Our goal, of course, is for the family to be healthy and remain together."

I don't say anything. I just sit there feeling like all the air has gone out of me. I have to live with people I barely know, in this house that isn't mine, and I won't even get to go home for at least half a year. That means I'll be here for the whole sixth grade, maybe longer. That can't happen. It just can't. And what about Darryl? He's my little brother. What is he supposed to do without me? He's probably been crying every night, if I know him.

Ms. Whitten looks in my eyes. "Madelyn," she says, "I don't know if you realize how serious this is. Darryl was beaten very badly, and there is ample evidence that this has been going on for quite some time." I want to look away, but she won't let me.

"But Daddy didn't mean to hurt Darryl that bad," I say. "He just wants us to mind."

"I know you love your father," she says, "and I'm not saying he's a bad person, but he has made some very poor choices. There's no law against a parent extending reasonable discipline to a child, but this does not fall into that category by any means. You know the difference between reasonable and unreasonable, don't you, Madelyn? Your father has a serious drinking problem and is unable or unwilling to control his behavior. Child abuse is not something the State takes lightly."

"Child abuse?" I whisper. I guess I knew that's what it was called, but this is the first time I've heard it applied to my own daddy.

"Yes, Madelyn. Child abuse is not just about locking a child up in a closet and starving him to death, even though that does happen. It's not just about burning a child with cigarettes or hot irons, although that happens too. It's also about discipline that gets out of control and causes grave harm to a minor child. That is what happened in your family, Madelyn, and it is of great concern to those of us who are charged with the protection of children. I'm sure you do love your father and mother, but what happened is illegal and wrong. Children are to be disciplined by their parents, but that does not mean beaten. Your brother was covered with bruises and welts and deep cuts, and you cannot go back home again until we are sure it is safe for you. Now, whether that is months or years, we don't know at this point. Do you understand what I am saying?"

I nod, not believing what I'm hearing. It could be years. I look away for a minute, and all I can see are things that don't belong to me. That's not my family's refrigerator, this isn't my mother's tablecloth, that's not our clock, those aren't our pictures. I'm not supposed to be here with these strange people. I want to go home.

"The Cochrans are happy to have you, Madelyn," Ms. Whitten is saying. "Darryl will stay where he is too, but you'll have regular visits with your mother and later your father, if he cooperates." She stacks up her papers and stuffs them into a folder, like she's fixing to leave. "Oh," she says, "I almost forgot. Your mother sent some of your winter clothes." She nods toward the corner, and I recognize Mama's brown suitcase sitting there. "Do you have any other questions, Madelyn?"

I think fast. I have to come up with something. This can't be the only choice. It just can't be. "What if Daddy moves out for a while?" I say, my words tumbling over each other, "What if he goes someplace and gets better? Somewhere that can help him not drink? Could we go home if he went to a place like that? And stayed there till he was well?"

Ms. Whitten pauses. "I don't know, Madelyn. That option hasn't been explored at this point. I suppose it would depend on the judge." She closes her briefcase and slips into her coat. "Do you have any questions, Mrs. Cochran?"

"No, but we do thank you for coming," Mrs. Cochran answers. I realize she hasn't said a word this whole time. "Madelyn is doing just fine, Ms. Whitten. We'll certainly keep you informed of any changes, but Margaret Ann and Jackie have really taken to her, and Robert and I enjoy having her here. She's an obedient, cooperative child who's not given us a moment's trouble."

Ms. Whitten looks pleased. "Madelyn, last week when I called, you said you were planning to make a card for your mother. Would you like for me to deliver it to her?"

"Yes," I say, "just a minute. It's in my room."

The card with the yellow roses is lying on my dresser. *Mama*, it begins. I read it over two times. Then I open my bottom drawer and stick it under my sweaters.

Ms. Whitten is waiting by the door with Mrs. Cochran when I get back. "Sorry," I say, "I forgot I left it at school."

"That's all right," she says. "I'll see you Thursday."

She gets in her car and backs out. I watch the street for a long time after she is gone.

Chapter 4

On my way to class the next day I decide to take the second set of stairs instead of the first, because then I can go right by Mr. Franklin's room. He is standing in the hallway holding his coffee mug when I pass. He smiles and says, "Hello, Miss Madelyn. How are you this morning?" and I say, "Fine."

Then I go on up the steps and sit at my desk and do my lessons, and nobody in the class says a word about what happened yesterday. I wonder what Mrs. Abernathy told them when I was gone, but I'm not about to ask. Jenna looks over at me and smiles once, but I don't know whether to smile back or not, so I don't. If she's being nice because she feels sorry for me, then no thank you. Besides, I've got too much on my mind to worry about making friends. I get out my workbook and pencil. We already did sentence diagramming at my old school, so I don't have to give it my full attention. That's a good thing, because I can't quit thinking about what Ms. Whitten said yesterday.

I don't know what I'll do if I don't get to go back home. I thought the police would have a long talk with Daddy and he'd see what he was doing and realize he was being too hard on Darryl. I thought if they scared him real good, being in uniforms and all, he'd quit. After all, he's a good citizen in every other way, as far as I can tell. He goes to work, drives the speed limit, keeps the yard mowed and even votes in most of the elections. Seems like he'd want to change if he knew he was doing wrong. Maybe Daddy was just afraid Darryl wouldn't take him serious if he didn't whip him for disobeying. Maybe he didn't realize he was overdoing it.

I don't know what to think. I'm just like the lucky penny I keep fingering in the pocket of my coat. One minute I decide that Daddy was trying to do right, and then the next minute it's like I turn that penny over and think that anybody ought to realize beating his son bloody is a terrible thing. I'm not but eleven, and I know that. Daddy has a mean streak a mile wide, and that's just the truth, like it or not. Why else would a grown man go after somebody who's sixty pounds soaking wet, just for getting a math problem wrong or forgetting his chores? In my whole life, I've never seen anything more awful than the hurt in Darryl's eyes after a beating. All he ever wanted was for Daddy to be proud of him. That's all he wanted. When I remember that, I don't feel a bit sorry for Daddy and what might happen to him. He ought to be whipped himself, and hard, to see how it feels.

And then there's Mama to think about. Darryl and me are getting picked up after school on Thursday, and we're meeting Mama at what Ms. Whitten calls a "neutral location." We haven't seen Mama since breakfast on the morning we got taken away. Ms. Whitten says she's doing all right, but I've got my doubts. Social workers might have a lot of experience with families flying apart every which a way, but regular people don't. *All right* is not how I would describe myself.

When I first went to the Cochrans, I cried my eyes out every night, but I know how to keep it quiet so nobody can hear me. I wonder if Mama cried too. Was she as scared as I was? What did she think when the police came to our house? Is she mad at us for telling?

43

I've never seen Mama get mad, come to think of it, although this might be the thing that puts her over the edge. She's always the one trying to keep everybody calm. If we're in the car and Daddy starts in, she can usually distract him by pointing out some pretty sight along the road. It's harder to do that at home, but she can sometimes get his attention by making a big deal over something she's taking out of the oven, like maybe a hot cherry pie that she puts ice cream on. She'll start interrupting Daddy, acting like she doesn't notice he's getting cranked up, and she'll be talking about umm, umm, this pie is going to be delicious, it sure turned out good this time, won't it taste wonderful with a big ole glass of cold milk, can you get plates and forks out Darryl, Madelyn you can pour the glasses, isn't it lucky we have a new gallon of vanilla ice cream in the freezer, oh I've been wanting a piece all day, this is Aunt Shirley's recipe and she makes the best pie, here have a seat, honey, I've got yours all ready.

If she can get him in a chair eating, then we're ok. She'll pat him and smile and get him to looking at her. Sometimes she'll even sit in his lap and kiss on him. Mama's slim and pretty, so if she can turn his attention to her, he might forget what he was so mad about.

I asked her once why she would go and pick a person who drank and got so excited. She said Daddy wasn't like that when they first got married. But then he got laid off and couldn't find work for nearly a year and a half, and that's when it all started, which is about the same time I was born. She said a lot of people drink and nothing bad happens, but with some people they just go crazy. They can't stop themselves from having more and more and more, and pretty soon they're doing things they wouldn't do if they were in their right minds. She says we should pray for him, and I have, but it hasn't done any good that I can tell.

* * *

At lunch Jenna gets in line beside me and sets her tray down by mine.

"Hi," she says. I say hi back.

Who knows? Maybe we can be friends after all.

* * *

Darryl is already in the car when Ms. Whitten picks me up on Thursday afternoon. "Maddie!" he yells out and throws the car door open. He hugs my neck, and it seems to me he's gotten taller in just these few weeks. He's wearing new pants and shoes and a big smile.

"What have you been up to?" I ask him. "Are you ok?"

"Yeah," he says, "come on and get in, we're going to see Mama." Like I didn't know.

I wave goodbye to Mrs. Cochran, who is standing on the porch with an everyday dress on and a dishtowel in her hand. I scoot in beside Darryl. Ms. Whitten looks back at us in the rear-view mirror. "How are you doing today, Madelyn?" she asks. I tell her I'm fine.

"Madelyn," Darryl whispers to me, "we have a dog at our house."

"What's Mama doing with a dog?" I ask. "She wouldn't ever let us have one before."

"No," he answers, "where I'm staying, with the Burgesses. There's a cat too, but it mostly belongs to Molly and Catherine. The dog sleeps in my room. His name is Dean and he's a yellow Labrador. You should see him, Maddie, he's huge!" His face is beaming. "I can't wait to tell Mama. Want to see what I made her?" He digs in his bag and pulls out a construction paper turkey, all orange and purple, yellow and red, with a string looped on the top. "This is to hang on the doorknob," he says, "and here's where I wrote the things I'm thankful for." He points to each

45

feather. *Flowers. Trees. Mama. Daddy. Sister. Air. Football. Dean. God. My new bike.* "Do you like it?" I say yes.

"And you know what else?" he asks.

"What?"

"I got a *100* on my math test Friday."

"You did?"

"Yes," he says. "Mr. Shelton, my math teacher, showed me how to do fractions, and it's not hard. I brought my paper. I'm going to get Mama to show Daddy."

"Well, good, Darryl," I say. "That's real good."

"Mrs. Burgess makes peanut butter milk shakes too. I'm going to get her to give Mama the recipe."

"That's easy," I say, "I can do that. All you do is put in ice cream and peanut butter and milk."

"No," Darryl says, "there's other stuff too." He looks out the window. In a minute he says to Ms. Whitten, "Is Daddy going to be there today?" I can't tell from his voice if he wants him to show up or not.

She looks back. "No," she says. "We think it's best to wait a while on that. Today is just the two of you and your mother."

We ride for a while, not talking, until we get to the Department of Human Services building at the county seat. We park around back and follow Ms. Whitten inside, down a long hall, and up the elevator to the fifth floor. Then she takes us into a room with a table, chairs, and a few old toys and tells us to wait. In a few minutes, she's standing in the doorway with Mama.

Mama sounds like she's choking and crying at the same time as she comes toward us with her arms open. "Madelyn! Darryl!" She falls on her knees and grabs us and holds on for the longest. Darryl's big grin turns upside down and he's crying too and has his face buried in her neck. "My babies, my babies," Mama says over and over. I feel like I'm standing outside myself, watching, wondering who these children are who haven't seen their own Mama in a month.

Finally, Ms. Whitten offers Mama a chair. She gets up and wipes her eyes and pulls Darryl down into her lap. "How's my baby?" she asks him, pushing his hair back and kissing his face all over. "Are you all right, baby? Are you ok?" She motions me into the chair beside her and pulls my head onto her shoulder. "Madelyn, my sweetheart, how are you, baby? Oh, how I've missed you." She holds us and rocks back and forth for a long time.

"Where's Daddy?" Darryl asks, pulling away and looking up at her. "Why didn't he come?"

"Baby, he couldn't come today," Mama answers.

"How's he doing?" I ask. My voice sounds strange and flat to me in this place.

"He's fine," Mama says. "He misses you too. And he feels so bad about what happened. He does. Darryl, he didn't mean to be so hard on you. He just loves you so much and wants you to do what he tells you and do good in school. He's so proud of you, Darryl. You know he loves you, don't you, baby? Don't you?"

Darryl looks down then and watches his hands for a long minute. "Yes ma'am," he says finally, but it comes out low.

"Darryl, you have to understand. Daddy works so hard and he just gets tired and doesn't feel like dealing with any foolishness when he gets home. You just need to do what he tells you and things will be all right. Pay attention when he's talking to you and go on and do what he says right then. You can do that, Darryl. You be a good boy and everything will be ok."

This time Darryl doesn't answer.

I almost forget Ms. Whitten sitting in the corner. She clears her throat. "Mrs. Bradshaw," she says, "Have you met with the parent training group yet?"

Mama nods, "That's where I'm going this evening. I started last week," she says.

"And Mr. Bradshaw?"

Mama lets out a sigh. "He's working late every day, still making up the time he missed, you know, a few weeks ago. He says he's going with me next time."

"That is a condition for the children's return," says Ms. Whitten. "The two of you, *both* of you, must attend group counseling. And he has to get help for his drinking."

"Yes, ma'am, I know," says Mama. "We'll do it. I promise we will." She hugs us to her again. "Oh, my babies," she whispers.

Then she asks us about where we're staying and if they're good to us and we tell her. Or rather, Darryl mostly tells her. She likes the door hanger he gives her and wants to hear all about the yellow dog and his new school. She promises to give the math paper to Daddy. Somehow I don't feel much like talking. I don't know what I thought she would say about Daddy, but I feel an empty place inside myself, kind of like I went to sit down and there was no chair under me. I just want to go somewhere else and curl up and sleep.

"Children," Ms. Whitten says after a while, "it's time to go. Tell your mother goodbye and you'll see her next time."

"When will that be?" asks Mama, slowly letting go of Darryl and me and standing up. She straightens her blouse with shaking hands.

"Three weeks from today," Ms. Whitten answers.

Mama starts crying and hugging us again, but not so tight this time. In a minute, she says, "Now, Madelyn, Darryl, don't worry. Daddy will be fine. As soon as he gets to feeling better, you can come home."

I stick my hands down into my coat pockets. "I'm ready to come home now," I say. "Can't Daddy go live some place else for a while until he quits drinking?" This time I am looking at Ms. Whitten, not Mama. "Can't he do that? I don't want to be in foster care. I want to go home."

"Madelyn," says Mama, "Daddy will get better. I promise." She turns toward the door, but I don't move.

"Can't you make him leave for a while," I ask, looking at her back now, "so we can come home? Can't you? He can get well some place else. I know they have hospitals that will help people stop drinking. He can get well and then come home, Mama. The judge will let him, I know he will. Don't make us stay with the foster people." My voice sounds louder than I expect in this bare room.

Ms. Whitten looks at Mama. "It's possible that we could approach the judge with that option, but Mr. Bradshaw would have to be willing to enter a facility. Even so, there is no guarantee the request would be granted."

Mama turns toward me. There is a look on her face that I don't understand, but it makes me feel scared and cold. I wonder if this is what it would feel like to have a policeman come to the house and say that my whole family had just gotten killed in a car wreck. "Madelyn," she says, "he is my husband and your father. I made a vow to stick by him in sickness and in health, and I'm going to keep that promise. He's doing the best he can. You'll be back home before you know it. You just need to be patient. I'm going to the classes they're having," she motions toward Ms. Whitten, "and your daddy knows he's got a few things to do too."

"A few things?" I say under my breath.

"What?" says Mama.

"Nothing," I answer.

She tries to hug me goodbye, but I just stand there, so she hugs Darryl and says she'll see us soon. Ms. Whitten goes with her out into the hall and tells us to wait, so we sit down at the table.

"Madelyn," Darryl looks at me, "are you mad at Mama?"

My mouth is too dry to say anything at first.

He looks worried. "Are you mad at me," he asks, "for telling?"

"No," I tell him, "you did right. I'm not mad at you."

Ms. Whitten is back soon and we ride the elevator down to the first floor and go on out to the parking lot. It's another cool, but not cold, day, and the leaves are dirty and wet under our feet. I start to scrape them off my shoes before I get in the car, but then I don't bother. Ms. Whitten takes me back first. The ride to the Cochrans seems long, and when I come in, they're having supper. I'm not hungry, so I go back to my room and lie down across the bed. Margaret Ann would have taken off her shoes and turned back the covers first, but I'm not Margaret Ann.

I stare up at the ceiling and watch it get darker and darker. It's only five-thirty, but night comes early this time of year. I keep the light off.

I think when I grow up, I am never getting married, not ever. I'm not taking a chance on somebody being one way before I marry him, and then changing right after. And if I did marry somebody, I sure wouldn't let him get away with mistreating my little boy or girl. If he did, he'd find his suitcases out on the porch the very first time. No, I wouldn't be taking his side. Not me, no sir. I'd tell him don't bother looking back, mister, cause you won't be coming this way again. If he did, I might just blow his head off. I hope God would forgive me for that.

Speaking of God, I remember what Mr. Cochran read at breakfast this morning. After he got done praying for the food, he read something out of his big Bible about two sparrows being sold for a penny and how not even one of them can fall to the ground without God knowing, and how God cares more about us than he does a bunch of birds. Today's the first time I've paid his

50

reading any attention, and the more I think about it, the more confused I get.

No matter how fine it sounds, I've got my doubts about things working exactly that way. I remember all those nights when I prayed Daddy would get well and he never did, when I prayed he would leave Darryl alone and he didn't, when I tried to be good and bad things still happened. I would not call that God watching out for people, by any means. He ought to be able to do better than that. And then there's today, seeing how Mama acted when I asked if she would make Daddy leave. She let me know right quick where I fit in the scheme of things. How could your own mama do you that way? How could she leave Darryl and me out here with nobody in the world to take care of us? What are we supposed to do? That's something I would like to ask God about. Why does he let grownups hurt children? Or leave them? Why does he say he cares about us if he's just going to sit up there in heaven and let everything go wrong?

Chapter 5

Friday morning is test-taking time in Mrs. Abernathy's room. Normally, I can make hundreds with my eyes closed, but that is not going to be the case today. The way I see it, I'm on my own now. Mama's not taking care of me and God's not taking care of me, so as far as I'm concerned, they can both kiss my natural white behind. I aim to do exactly as I please. Miss Madelyn Bradshaw, perfect student, has left the building.

When the teacher calls out *spaghetti* on the spelling test, I leave out the *h* on purpose. I put *inconsiderite* for *inconsiderate* and change a letter or two in every single word she says. At first, my hands are shaking and my stomach feels cold and twisted, like I'm about to throw up, and I don't know if I can make myself keep on. I've never made under a B in my life, and this is going to turn out an F for sure. But the more I think about Mama, the madder I get. I put *lagune* for *lagoon,* and I'm bearing down so hard on my pencil that the lead breaks and I have to get out a new one. I've never had nerve enough to be this bad before, but I have to say, there's a satisfaction in it that runs clear through me. I do the English and social studies tests the same way. The more wrong answers I put, the better I feel. By the time I'm done with all of them, I could just about crow, I feel so good. For the first time this week I raise my chin and look people square in the eye. At lunch, I even smile at

Lindsay and her snotty little friends, which sure enough gives them something to talk about. *The foster child is rising from the ashes,* I think.

During math, I put my hand up for the first time since I've been here. I'm sure that surprises the whole class, as they all turn around to look. Mrs. Abernathy calls on me and I give a wrong answer on purpose. She tries to give me another chance, thinking I need help, but I don't. If the answer is 45, I say 47. If it's 223, I say 253. She looks kind of desperate, like she's trying hard for me to get it right, but I keep messing it up. Nobody laughs or says a word. I guess they remember what happened with the hair color chart.

Science is even better. When Mrs. Abernathy asks for volunteers to read parts of Chapter 4 out loud, I raise my hand. I start where she tells me, but then I keep mispronouncing words, even though I've been ahead of my grade in reading since I was six years old. Also, I act like I'm losing my place so that I have to start over. I do that three or four times before she gives up and moves on to somebody else. I've got better sense than to smile on the outside, but inside I'm grinning fit to beat the band.

I start to like this new Madelyn, the one who does things wrong and enjoys it. I lean back and cross my arms over my chest and just dare Mrs. Abernathy to call on me. I think I'm making her nervous, which feels good, I have to say. A couple of times, Jenna gives me funny looks, but I don't care.

By 2:00, I'm about worn out from trying to be bad. It takes some extra effort when you're so used to doing it the other way around. I'm glad we're heading down to Mr. Franklin' room for the last hour of the day. He was so nice to me on Tuesday that I don't feel like causing him any trouble. We take our books and coats so we'll be ready for dismissal, and Mrs. Abernathy leads the way.

Mr. Franklin has that music playing in the background again, and I soften up some just walking through his door. He has stacks of magazines on all the tables, and he tells us we're going to start on our collages today. First of all, he tells us what a collage is and shows us some samples. Then he says we're making ones that illustrate aspects of our character. Like if we think we're adventuresome, we can find pictures of somebody climbing a mountain or sailing around the world. If we are gentle, we might want to show a person holding a kitten. He says to cut out words too and use those to help explain or emphasize our qualities. He also says to spend some time thinking about our character traits first, but most people just want to get straight to the magazines.

One thing I like about art, it doesn't matter if your picture is different from somebody else's. It's still good, as long as you don't just slop something down. For instance, when I drew that charcoal face last week, it didn't look anything like Laura's or Katie's or Sarah's. I drew a girl looking out from behind a tree, and I made her hair look like it was part of the birds and the branches. Her eyes were a little too scared-looking for my taste, but I bet I could fix that if I had some more time to work on her.

For my collage, I decide I'm hunting for words and pictures to go along with *brave* and *smart*. If I were at my old school, I might have picked *friendly* too, but I don't think that applies here. I cut out a picture of a mountain lion and stick that in my folder. That can stand for *brave*. There's a girl on a high dive too, which is a brave place to be, and then there's somebody holding a snake behind the jaws. I almost don't get the snake one, but then I remember Mr. Franklin didn't say a person actually had to *do* these things. He says they are just meant to illustrate.

Finding pictures for *smart* is a little harder. I cut out a set of encyclopedias and then some eggs, which can stand for being an egghead. Eggs are also brain food, I read somewhere. Then I find a picture of a woman reading. She's at the beach, which is a place I've never been, but I get her anyway. I can always cut around her and leave out the sand and water. There's a globe on the next page too, which can go with *smart* if I can't find anything better.

I'm so busy squirreling away pictures I don't even notice the woman who comes in, until she laughs. She's got a little girl with her who looks to be about five, and they're holding hands. Mr. Franklin is smiling at them both, and he picks up the girl and gives her a hug and kiss, and she puts her arms around his neck. The only thing I can think is, these people must be Mr. Franklin's family. I ask Jenna and she says yes, they are. I can't remember the last time Daddy hugged Darryl or me like that, and it makes my stomach hurt some to watch it. Or at least it would, if I wasn't so mad at him.

The bell is about to ring, so Mr. Franklin tells us to clean up and get ready to go home. He says we'll finish the collages next time. When we are dismissed, I take my time about leaving. My eyes are hungry to see how Mr. Franklin holds his child. She grins at him, and he laughs and wiggles his eyebrows. Mrs. Franklin, if that's her name, moves around the room picking up scissors and putting them up in the cabinet. Her voice is gentle like the music, and she looks as soft and comfortable as a pillow. I wish God had given me a family like this, where people like each other.

I don't even notice that I'm the last person in the room until Mr. Franklin looks over and smiles at me. "Madelyn," he says, "let me introduce you to my wife Pauline, and my daughter Ellen." He puts the little girl down, and she goes to help her mother.

Pauline Franklin smiles, and I am so embarrassed for staring that I almost forget to say I'm pleased to meet them. When I finally do, I add, "Some people call me Maddie. You can too. If you want, that is."

"Well then," says Mrs. Franklin, smiling and taking my hand in both of hers, "I'm very glad to meet you, Maddie."

I'm pretty sure I ought to get my stuff and clear out then so they can be alone, but then Mr. Franklin says, "Madelyn, would you like to put the folders away?"

I say OK, and he hands me the box for our class. "They go alphabetically, by last name," he says. I'm good at putting things in order, so it only takes me a few minutes. I tell him I walk home from school and am not in any hurry, so if there is anything else he wants me to do, I'll be happy to help. He offers to call Mrs. Cochran and tell her I'm staying late, so I let him.

I end up helping Mrs. Franklin mix paints for next week's classes. Then we make letters for the bulletin board. Ellen wants to help too, but she is not what I would call a good cutter. When I was her age, I could use scissors a lot better than she does. I make sure that when I finish each one, I put it in my own pile so ours don't get mixed in together. I wouldn't want the Franklins to think I do sloppy work. I expect Mrs. Franklin to say something to Ellen about being careful like me, but she doesn't.

Mrs. Franklin asks me about myself and where I'm from, and I tell her. Now, I don't tell her *why* I'm living with the Cochrans, only that I am. She doesn't appear to be the nosy type, as she doesn't try to pry anything else out of me. Besides, I get the feeling she's just being friendly and doesn't think any less of me for not being in my own home with my own mama and daddy.

We finally get finished, and it's time to leave. Mr. Franklin reminds everybody to wrap up good since the temperature has dropped off a good bit today. I get my coat on and we go on outside. They offer to take me home, but I only live a few houses down so I tell them I don't mind walking. The real reason is, I think it would feel strange to be in a car with them when it's just supposed to be only their family. That's different from being in the classroom where I have to go anyway.

* * *

I almost forget about the first part of the day where I gave all those wrong answers, but I get reminded the minute I walk in the door. Mrs. Cochran is sitting at the kitchen table holding the phone to her ear, and she motions me to sit down.

"I don't understand it either," Mrs. Cochran says, "Up to now, she's been making all *A*'s." She pauses to listen. "Every single one?" she asks. "No, I don't, but I'll speak with her about it." She stops again. "Yes, Mrs. Abernathy, thank you so much for calling. I assure you, we will get to the bottom of this." Mrs. Cochran sets the phone down and looks at me.

"Well, Madelyn?" she says. "I'm sure you know what that was about. Your teacher says you failed every test you took today and couldn't seem to read a word when she called on you in class. Would you like to explain what happened?"

I was feeling pretty good from being with the Franklins, but now yesterday's visit with Mama comes rushing back, and I feel angry and backed into a corner all over again. "No," I answer.

She looks surprised and more stern than I've ever seen her. In addition to being mad at Mama, now this lady I barely know is trying to act like she's my boss. Maybe that works with Margaret Ann and Jackie, but I'm not a part of this family, and I don't have to do what she says. "Young lady," Mrs. Cochran goes on. "In this house, you are expected to do your schoolwork exactly as your teacher tells you. Mrs. Abernathy says you were not even trying today. What do you have to say for yourself?"

"Nothing," I answer.

Mrs. Cochran's eyes flash once before she catches herself and calms down. "Then you can sit right here until you can give me an answer." She gets up from the table and goes back over to the stove to stir something.

I don't know anything that could happen to me that hasn't happened already, so I get up myself and head on back to my room.

"Madelyn!" Mrs. Cochran's voice is sharp and firm, but I don't turn around. I go in my room, throw my books and coat on the floor, and flop down on the bed. Mrs. Cochran is standing in the doorway before I can say Jack Robinson.

"Young lady," she says, "you do not get up when I tell you to sit still. Do you understand me? Now you get back in that kitchen and stay there until you can give me a respectful answer about why you failed every test you took today." I don't move. "Come on," she says, but I don't. I just turn over, face the wall, and put the pillow over my head. If I were at home, I'd be wondering when the belt was about to fall. But I'm not at home.

I can feel Mrs. Cochran still standing there, but she's not going to do anything. I'm under the protection of the State, so she can't lay a hand on me. I found that out from a girl who used to know somebody in foster care. Finally, I hear her walk away. I might not get any dinner tonight, but I can always sneak in the kitchen later and find something. Miss Madelyn Bradshaw can take care of herself.

* * *

Saturday is cold and rainy. I stay in my room the whole day and eat cookies and raisins and carrots from a sack that I hid in my closet the night before, after everybody went to bed. Mrs. Cochran calls me for meals, but I tell her I'm not hungry, so she doesn't bother me. I think I make her tired. Margaret Ann is working on a project, and Jackie is at his friend's house, so it's pretty quiet around here. Mr. Cochran always spends Saturdays working on his sermon down at the church, so that's one less person to worry about.

Last night, through the wall, I heard Mr. and Mrs. Cochran talking, but I couldn't make out the words. I don't care. The worst they can do is tell Ms. Whitten, and what's she going to do? Tell Mama? Well, good, that's what I had in mind to start with. Maybe she'll think twice about making her children live with strangers.

Sunday rolls around again, and I go on out to breakfast. I'm about to starve for some real food, and they're sure not about to bring it to me. Nobody says anything about Friday or yesterday, which I consider a good sign. I even get ready on time and head on over to church with Margaret Ann. Jackie spent the night at his cousin's house and won't be back until sometime this evening.

Margaret Ann looks over at me a couple of times as we're walking through the parking lot, but all she says is, "Madelyn, is everything ok?" And all I say is yes.

During Sunday School, I hide out in the bathroom because I just can't stand being in the same room with Lindsay and her ugly, stupid face. If anybody asks, I'll just say my stomach was hurting, which wouldn't be a total lie.

When the bell finally rings, I go on out and look for Margaret Ann and follow her up to the second row of the church. I don't know why we have to be on public display. My guess is that we're supposed to be setting a good example for the congregation, but I for one am not interested.

We go through a few songs, but I only pretend like I'm singing. I heard once that if you say *watermelon watermelon watermelon* over and over, your mouth looks like you're really singing, so I try it out and it works. That's a real handy thing to know, in case you're ever up in front of people in a school program and forget the words. I don't close my eyes during the prayers either. If anybody says something about it, I can just ask them why *their* eyes were open.

Then Mr. Cochran gets up there and pulls his sermon notes out of his big black Bible. He looks out over the audience, probably checking to see who didn't show up today, then starts in.

"Brothers and sisters," he says, "we come here today in the presence of Almighty God to worship and praise His holy name. And why, you ask, why should we gather together each and every Lord's Day, when our friends out in the world treat this day as no different from any other?"

I bet if he called for a show of hands, nobody would be asking any such thing. You come because somebody makes you, and somebody made *them,* and so on and so forth, on back to the beginning of time. I could have told him that.

"Friends, we meet together because God commands that we do so. As our Father in Heaven, He issues laws and rulings for the good of His household. And we *are* His household, His chosen and holy people who proclaim His glory, majesty, and dominion forever and ever, Amen. He is our Father and we are His children, brothers and sisters."

I wonder whatever happened to the Father who was waiting and watching on the portals. That was the one I used to like. This one sounds like somebody you might call Your Honor.

I've decided neither one is the kind of father I want anyway. I thought God was supposed to be holding the whole world in his hands. If he's as strong and mighty as they say at church, he ought to be putting a stop to bad things like people killing and robbing each other. If I was him, there wouldn't be anybody going to bed hungry or needing medicine and not getting it. Nobody would be starting wars, and if somebody dumped their newborn baby in a trashcan, I'd put a lightning bolt straight through their heart in a New York minute. It seems to me he's not paying attention to some great big problems, so it doesn't come as a surprise that he's slacking up on the little ones too.

I don't know why I thought he'd do something about our family. You can't see him, you can only talk to him, so maybe he's not even there. Preachers say he is, but that doesn't make it so. Maybe nobody is watching out for us. Maybe we're just here by ourselves and good luck.

"Our Father who art in heaven..." Mr. Cochran is praying now.

Speaking of art, Mr. Franklin is the kind of father I would prefer, if I could pick. I like his story about the two vases he told me that very first day we talked. He said he liked them both just because he made them, even though in my opinion the blue one was a lot prettier. He said that didn't matter, and that they were both worth the same to him. Some people might say God is the same way, but I don't know that I agree. Seems to me that he takes care of some people and can't be bothered with the rest of us. If I was as good as Margaret Ann, I could probably ask him a real big favor and he'd jump right on it.

All this talking and thinking about fathers is making me want to scream. My nerves haven't been too good lately anyway. I wish Mr. Cochran would change the subject, but it looks like he's going to squeeze every last drop out of it that he can. I can't turn all the way around, but I can sneak a glance over my shoulder every once in a while, and sure enough, this place is packed with fathers. They're probably soaking all this in and being so pleased with themselves they could pop. Goody for them is all I can say. I wouldn't give two cents for a father, in heaven or otherwise.

At lunch Mr. Cochran makes a special point of praying for the forgiveness of our sins. I know he's talking about me, but I don't care.

I spend the afternoon alone in my room again. I could go be with Margaret Ann, but I just don't feel like company. I read my library book for a while, but mostly I spend the day wondering how you can love a person and hate them at the same time. Sometimes my heart hurts so bad remembering Daddy's smile, but other times I could strike him dead. It's the same with Mama. I want to crawl up in her lap and let her hold me and rock me like a baby. I want to put my arms around her neck and snuggle up to her soft, sweet body and hear her sing. But a minute later I want to stand up and shake her as hard as I can. And then there's Darryl. He's happy as a lark with two brand new sisters and a big yellow dog. I'm not there to watch after him, and it seems like he doesn't even care. Somebody ought to tell him that those people are not his real family.

I'm a mess. I don't know who to love anymore. I just keep turning that penny over and over in my hand.

Chapter 6

On Monday morning I pass by Mr. Franklin' room on the way up to my class. He's standing in the hall with his coffee cup as usual, and as usual he smiles and says, "Good morning, Miss Madelyn." Since that might be the only good thing that happens to me today, it's worth the extra walking.

When Mrs. Abernathy gets us started on grammar, I know I'm going to be giving the wrong answers again. At first my stomach feels knotted up thinking about it, like it did last Friday, and for a minute, I wonder if I'm going to need the bathroom pass. But once I get going good, it's all right. Truth is, making A's is easy. Daddy was always so proud of my report cards. He always laid out a dime for every A I got and bragged on how smart I was. It felt good to see him so happy. But now, thinking how Ms. Whitten came right out and called him a child abuser, I feel sick and mad. He didn't give Darryl any dimes, that's for sure. He's sure not worth me trying to do good, and neither is Mama.

Mrs. Abernathy comes around to pick up our papers twenty minutes later. She stands by my desk for the longest, looking at my worksheet where I've circled any old thing without even reading it. She says, "Madelyn?" and starts to say something else, but James asks her a question and by the time I look up, she's not paying attention anymore. She moves on down the row, and I bend over my paper again, but I can't see as it matters what I put down and whether it's right or wrong.

Math, reading, science, social studies, it's all the same. Part of me is scared I'll fail the sixth grade if I keep this up, but the rest of me doesn't care. I could disappear right now, and nobody would miss me, that's for sure. Mrs. Cochran doesn't like me, my teacher doesn't care about me, Darryl doesn't need me anymore, and everybody thinks I'm dirty and bad.

I do a few more assignments without even trying, and the more wrong answers I put down, the stronger and more awake I feel. I can't make Mama do right, and I can't make Daddy quit drinking, but I can do this. I can put down whatever answers I want, I can walk out when I feel like it, I can say anything that comes in my head, I can fly out a window if I have a mind to. When Mrs. Abernathy has us do compositions about ocean life, I write about the Rocky Mountains. When we do long division, I mix up the hundreds and thousands places. I raise my hand a few times and give wrong answers just so Mrs. Abernathy won't think she scared me by tattling to Mrs. Cochran. I don't write down any of the homework because I don't plan to do it. I am Miss Madelyn Bradshaw, and I don't have to answer to anybody, so there.

The whole week is like that. Mr. Franklin says hello in the morning, and I do what I want the rest of the day. I can tell the teacher is put out with me. She takes me out in the hall and tries talking to me a couple of times and tells me what excellent work I had been doing and would I please tell her what is going on, but I don't. I just stand there with my arms crossed and look at something over her shoulder till she shuts up. She'll probably call the Cochrans again after our tests on Friday, but if she thinks that's going to do any good, she can think again.

Jenna smiles at me a few times, but I don't need her either. When she sits down by me at lunch on Monday, I don't have much to say to her, and on Tuesday, I'm not saying anything at all. Come Wednesday, she's sitting somewhere else, and that's fine by me.

Thursday is when it all hits the fan. Somehow I end up right in front of Lindsay in the lunch line. I'm getting my tray and moving forward a little, ready to reach over and grab a carton of milk, when I feel something in my back. Lindsay is pushing her tray into me. At first, I think maybe she isn't meaning to, but I should have known better. I take a step, but so does she, and she presses the tray into my back again, harder.

"Stop it, you idiot!" I hiss over my shoulder, but she doesn't. Then I see two of her friends watching us and laughing, and I guess I just lose my mind. I whirl around as fast as I can and shove the tray right up into her face. She stumbles backward, slips on the green beans, and falls, her legs sprawled out every which a way, mashed potatoes and chicken all over her fancy new clothes. Blood is pouring from her nose, and her mouth is wide open like she's going to cry, but nothing comes out. The lunch line is instantly silent, and it's just me standing over her, breathing hard, with my fists clenched up.

"You. Leave. Me. Alone!" I shout into the silence. It seems like forever that everybody is just frozen in one spot, with the only sound being me taking in big gulps of air, but then I see a movement in the corner of my eye and here comes one of the cafeteria monitors. In a second, she is in between Lindsay and me.

"Stand by that wall!" she orders, and I back up and watch her help Lindsay to her feet. She's crying now, the big baby, and she goes off with some teacher's arm around her shoulders. Then the monitor lady takes me by the arm and heads out toward the office. I jerk away. Nobody needs to be snatching at me like that.

"Young lady, what in the world are you thinking?" she asks. I don't know if she expects an answer or not, but she's not getting one. I got nothing to say.

In a minute, I am sitting outside the principal's office door, and she is inside telling him all about it. The secretary goes in and out a couple of times, but she doesn't say anything to me. After a while, Mr. Raiford says to come in, and I do, but he can't make me talk. I flop down in one of the big straight-backed chairs in front of his desk with my arms crossed over my chest. The lunch monitor sits in the other one.

Mr. Raiford is studying a folder on his desktop and doesn't say anything for a few minutes. He is tall, nearly bald, wears glasses, and looks sort of like a llama in the face. Finally, he looks up, and I stare right back at him. If he thinks he can scare me, he'd better think again.

"Madelyn Denise Bradshaw," he says. "Is that correct?"

He doesn't wait for an answer, just picks up one of the papers in the folder. "You're new here at Fulton, aren't you? We have the records from your previous school, and it appears, Madelyn, that you have been an excellent student in the past." He runs his finger down the page. "Honor roll, grades K-5. Superior marks in conduct. Complimentary comments from all your teachers. Excellent test scores in every subject." He pauses for a minute, leans forward, and folds his hands together. "And yet you come to Fulton, to a new school where you ought to be concerned with making a favorable impression, and you attack another student in the cafeteria. Am I correct?"

I don't answer.

"This is your opportunity to explain yourself," he continues. "If there are reasons for such outrageous conduct, I am prepared to listen. If you choose not to provide any additional information, I will assume that my impressions are accurate." He waits for a long minute, but I don't say anything. I go from looking at him to looking out the window behind his desk. It's the middle of November now, and there aren't many leaves left on the trees outside, just a few raggedy brown ones hanging on for dear life and refusing to fall. It's hard to believe they were so fresh and green just a few months ago or that they ever will be again. They just look dead to me. I could almost get lost thinking about them, but Mr. Raiford has to start talking again.

"I feel certain that physical violence was not permitted at Oak Valley, and you can rest assured it is forbidden here at Fulton as well. I cannot fathom the motive behind such an incident as occurred today. I am well acquainted with Lindsay Sutton's family, the other child involved in this altercation. They are upstanding community members. Lindsay has attended Fulton Elementary since third grade and has always been a model student. I find it extremely difficult to believe that she would have any part in provoking such an assault." He clears his throat and picks up another sheet of paper. "Before you came in, I took the liberty of requesting from your teacher a listing of your current grades. It seems that you are performing far below grade level. In fact, your assignments for the past several days have yielded a number of *D*'s and *F*'s. Your prior performance here and at your previous school indicates that you are capable of academic excellence. Perhaps there is something going on that you have yet to tell us about."

He looks at me like he expects me to say something, but I don't. After a minute, he shrugs his shoulders and nods toward the lunch monitor. "Have Madelyn wait in the outer office, Miss Tinsley. I'll have Mrs. Cochran to pick her up for the remainder of the day."

I get up and go out by myself. I don't need somebody leading me like I'm a kindergarten baby. I sit down on one of the chairs and wait. There's a kid out here with a thermometer in his mouth too, and I sit down right beside him. I hope I catch whatever he has. I hope I get sick and die.

Mrs. Cochran is at the school in just a few minutes. The secretary sends her straight to Mr. Raiford's office, and he shuts the door. Half an hour later, they come out. I wonder what all they talked about, but nobody tells me anything. The secretary buzzes Mrs. Abernathy and tells her to send down my stuff, and we go get in the car.

Mrs. Cochran cranks the car and then sits staring out the front window not saying anything. The end of her nose is red, and her eyes are watering from the cold. I start to say, how about turning on the heat, but I decide not to. Finally, she backs out and heads down the street. We drive right past the house into the church parking lot, and she says to get out and follow her in, that we're going to speak with Mr. Cochran. I think about just staying where I am, but I'm freezing half to death so I go on into the building with her. It's a whole lot warmer once we get inside, and I follow her down the hall to the office. The secretary shows us in. Mr. Cochran is at his desk with books and papers stacked up everywhere. He doesn't look too happy about being interrupted. And he sure doesn't look happy to see me.

"Robert," Mrs. Cochran says, standing very straight, "we seem to be having a problem. I was just called to the school to pick up Madelyn. It appears that she pushed Lindsay Sutton down at lunch and bloodied her nose. You know Lindsay, Tom and Greta's daughter. The principal spoke with Madelyn, and she apparently did it for no reason. We've already discussed how low her grades have been for the past week, and her teacher says they're not getting any better. I don't know what's going on, but it has to stop right here and now."

"Young lady," Mr. Cochran says, taking off his glasses and cleaning them with his handkerchief, "these are some very serious things your mother is saying."

I am up and screaming before I know it: "She's not my mother! And you're not my father! You can't tell me what to do!"

They are both stock-still for a second, just staring at me. Then Mr. Cochran speaks, "Hold on, young lady, you just calm yourself down. You're right. We are not your parents, but you are in our care at the moment, and you will obey us. You will also follow the school's rules and do the work your teacher assigns. There will be no more fighting. The Suttons, including Lindsay, are esteemed members of our church, and you will show them the consideration they deserve. While you are in our home, you are subject to the rules of our household, and that includes respecting our authority and the authority of the school." He raises one black eyebrow, but I just glare at him.

"I don't have to do what you say," I answer.

"I'm afraid that's where you're mistaken," Mr. Cochran answers. "You do indeed have to do as we say. We are your foster parents, and you are in our care."

"Says who?" I ask. "I don't have to stay here."

"The State determines that, young lady. You do not."

"Well, the State can go to hell!"

"Lorraine," says Mr. Cochran stiffly, rising from his chair, "I think it best that you take Madelyn on home. If there's anything else to discuss, we can deal with it this evening."

I stomp down the hall and outside. I'm so hot the air feels good when it hits my face, and I march up the hill to the house while Mrs. Cochran pulls the car into the driveway. She lets us in and I go straight to my room and shut the door hard. That stupid Lindsay, that stupid school, this stupid house, my stupid life. "I hate you!" I yell as loud as I can. "I hate you! And I hate this stupid family! You're all stupid!" I open the door and slam it as hard as I can three times and then lock it. "Stupid! Stupid! Stupid!"

I grab the bottle of perfume off the dresser and throw it against the wall. It breaks and I'm glad. I smash the yellow ceramic bird too and then crush it some more with my shoes. Then I pull out a drawer and slam it against the headboard of the bed. Crack! There are pieces everywhere. I hear Mrs. Cochran knocking and yelling for me to let her in, but I don't. I grab my red and black markers, one in each hand, and mark all over the walls. Up, down, zigging and zagging and slashing, hard, hard, hard. All over, red and black and red. I hate you, I hate you, I hate you! I write hard up and down my arms and all over my face. I bash in the mirror with the lamp, and the glass cuts my hand.

I am standing there, staring at the blood dripping on my shirt, when the door bursts open and there is Mr. Cochran. Mrs. Cochran is behind him with both hands over her mouth.

"God in Heaven!" says Mr. Cochran, "God in Heaven!" He backs out, I hear him on the phone, and before I know it, the police are here. Mrs. Cochran washes my cut, which turns out not to be anything to worry about. It's not long before Ms. Whitten pulls up. She sits me down at the kitchen table and asks me questions, and so do the police, but I don't know what to tell them. I'm hurting so bad I don't even know where it's coming from anymore. And I'm tired, so tired all I want to do is sleep and sleep and sleep. I put my head down because I just can't think anymore, I can't answer questions, I can't stay awake. They finally put me in Margaret Ann's bedroom and go into the other room to talk. I hear their voices, the deep ones of Mr. Cochran and the police officers, and the higher ones of Mrs. Cochran and Ms. Whitten, but I don't hear the words. I pull the ruffled yellow comforter over my head and sleep.

* * *

When I wake up later, my hair is all sweaty and matted to my cheeks, and it takes a minute to remember what happened. I sit up and listen, and I can still hear voices in the next room. The police are gone, but Ms. Whitten hasn't left. If I wasn't dying to use the bathroom, I'd stay here and pretend I'm still asleep, but I can't wait. I open the door quietly and slip down the hall, but then I forget and flush, so everybody knows I'm up. Ms. Whitten's head pops around the corner and tells me to come on back in the kitchen and have a seat. I notice the clock says four-thirty, and I wonder where Jackie and Margaret Ann are, but I don't want to ask.

Mr. Cochran's sipping coffee, and there's a plate of cookies on the table. I'm hungry, since I didn't get any lunch, but I don't reach for anything. Mrs. Cochran's eyes are red like she's been crying, and she doesn't look at me. Ms. Whitten's papers are spread out in front of her.

"Are you feeling better, Madelyn?" Ms. Whitten asks. I shrug, and we sit in silence, waiting for me to answer, I guess. Then she clears her throat. "Madelyn," she says, "The Cochrans think it is best for you—and for their family—if we arrange another placement for you." I must look shocked, but she keeps on. "Sometimes that happens in foster care. A child is not a good match for the family, or else incidents occur that make it impossible to continue the arrangement." She stares directly at me over her reading glasses, but I look away. "There are occasions in which a foster family serves as a stepping stone to a more appropriate placement. In this case, the best option appears to be making a move to another home."

I stare at her. I'm leaving, I think. She's going to make me go live somewhere else. Not home. Not with Mama, but with some other family I don't even know, maybe in some other town. I would have to change schools again, and no telling what kind of foster home I'd land in next. I've heard some of them can be bad.

"Why can't I just stay here?" I ask, after a minute. My voice comes out sounding small and weak. It's not that I want to stay, exactly. It's just that I don't want to go anywhere new and start all over.

"Plans change," Ms. Whitten answers, closing her folder. "It is too late in the day today to make the switch, but I will be in contact tomorrow as soon as I can find an opening for you. The holidays are not the best time of year to be altering a placement, but I will do my best to see that this situation is relieved as soon as possible." She gets up, shakes hands with the Cochrans, and they all move toward the front door. "Thank you so much," I hear her say, "and please do not feel that the department considers this a failure on your part. We understand the pressures families face when dealing with troubled children, and we certainly understand your concern over the events of today. I assure you I will give you a call as soon as I can locate another family willing to take a child this age."

I hear the door open and close, and then Mr. Cochran's recliner squeaks in the den, so he's probably going in there to take a nap or catch up on his reading. Mrs. Cochran comes back into the kitchen.

"What about Darryl?" I ask, "Can I go stay with him?"

Mrs. Cochran sighs. She's not standing so tall and stern anymore. I guess she feels bad about not being able to make an eleven-year-old girl mind her. "Ms. Whitten made a call to his foster family while you were sleeping, and it's not a possibility at this time."

"Why?" I ask.

"I don't know, Madelyn. It just isn't." She starts pulling things out of the refrigerator, and I can tell the conversation is over.

I pick a couple of apples out of a bowl on the counter and go back to my room. I don't imagine I'm going to be welcome at the supper table. The door to my room is wide open, and there's a hole in it, probably from where Mr. Cochran smashed through it. Big stripes of black and red are all over the walls, and there are nails and pieces of wood on the bedspread. It's a mess, for sure. I guess I don't blame them for kicking me out. If somebody trashed my house, I'd probably get rid of them too. I put the broken drawer and the splinters over in the corner and pick up as much of the glass as I can, but there's nothing I can do about the paint job. I save all the pieces of the yellow bird that I can find and dump them in an empty shoebox in my closet. Maybe I can glue it back together. I even crawl way under the bed looking to see if I missed any slivers.

After I'm done, I go to the bathroom and scrub and scrub my face and all up my arms. The soap doesn't work so great, so I get the scouring powder and rub it in hard. I about take the skin off my face, but I don't care. The cut on my hand burns something awful, even though it's just a little place.

In a few minutes I hear the front door open and then Mrs. Cochran talking to Margaret Ann and Jackie in the kitchen. I can't make out what she's saying, but I'm sure I don't come off all that wonderful. I can hear Jackie crying all the way in here, and my heart about breaks in two. I sure wouldn't let anybody know it though. My insides are all a mess, and I feel so bad I could die.

God, can't you make the hurting stop? That is, if you're not too tied up watching out for all the falling sparrows.

Chapter 7

Whether it's about the police coming to the Cochrans or what happened with Lindsay, I don't know, but the minute I set foot inside the school on Friday, it seems like everybody is staring at me. I go down the hall toward Mr. Franklin's room like always, knowing this is probably my last time to say hello to him.

He's in his usual spot with his hands wrapped around his coffee cup. "Good morning, Miss Madelyn," he says like he always does. I take a few steps past his doorway, but then I stop and come back. I don't know why, but I want him to know that I'm leaving.

"Mr. Franklin," I say, "I won't be here anymore after today. I just wanted to say thank you for being nice to me."

He starts to say something back, but all of a sudden I feel like I'm going to cry, so I spin around and run up the stairs to my classroom. Stupid, stupid, stupid. By now I ought to know better than to care about people. Something bad always happens when you do. Or else you have to leave them. Better just to stay away and forget about them.

I take my seat in Mrs. Abernathy's class. She starts in on adjectives and adverbs, but I don't hear much of what she's saying. I keep thinking about what happened yesterday and how everything has changed all of a sudden. I wonder where I'll be tonight, wonder who I'll be living with and how long I'll be there. What will I say to them? Where will I go to school? I feel so tired, all the way down to my heart, like somebody is sitting on my chest pushing all the air out.

I'm sure Mr. and Mrs. Cochran won't miss me, but Margaret Ann might, and Jackie. I told them goodbye this morning, and I gave Jackie my box of markers. Except for the red and black ones, they're in good shape, and he needed some new ones. Some of his were dried up. Margaret Ann hugged me, and I whispered "I'm sorry" in her ear, but I don't know if she heard.

When I get back to the Cochrans in the afternoon, Ms. Whitten's red car is in the driveway. She calls me into the kitchen where she and Mrs. Cochran are sitting at the table, in the same spots as they were last night, come to think of it. I sit down too.

Ms. Whitten asks how school was today and I say ok, but I know that's not why she's here. "Madelyn," she says, taking off her reading glasses and looking at me, "you must know how difficult it is to find another placement quickly under these circumstances. I made numerous calls around the county, and either the homes are full, or they prefer to wait until after the holidays to accept a placement. It's such a busy season, and so many people are traveling this time of year." I wonder if she's going to make the Cochrans keep me, whether they want to or not. I'm not sure she can do that, but it sounds to me like she might be headed that direction.

"In a case where there has been a major disruption at school, we prefer to place a child in a different educational environment so that he or she has a fresh start. However, we have limited options for the reasons I've outlined, and that doesn't appear to be a possibility. Since there were no available spots with our current foster families, we went back through our records of homes that had closed within the last two years, but. I'm afraid there are no placement possibilities in that category either." She looks down at her paperwork and puts her glasses back on. "I've discussed this with Mr. and Mrs. Cochran, and they have agreed, albeit reluctantly, to give you another chance. You understand, of course, that the State is now responsible for the property damage you've inflicted." She frowns hard over the top of her glasses. "And let me say this. You are a very lucky young lady that you're being allowed to stay. Our only other option would be a juvenile detention facility."

Jail? Does she mean jail? I'm thinking. I can barely breathe, but I don't let on. In fact, I look at the clock on the wall behind her and act like she hasn't said anything at all.

"I'm sure she's sorry about the whole incident," says Mrs. Cochran, clearing her throat, "and I'm sure she'll do better from now on."

"Let's hope so," says Ms. Whitten. "Otherwise, we'll have quite a problem on our hands." She turns to me. "Do you have anything to say, Madelyn?"

"Yes ma'am," I mumble, "I'm sorry about, you know, the room."

"Well then," says Ms. Whitten, standing up and putting on her coat. Mrs. Cochran follows her to the front door, and I go on back down the hall. I figure I better start trying to scrub the markers off the walls before I end up in jail. I didn't know the police would arrest eleven-year-old kids.

* * *

After that awful day, I decide to start doing better in school. I don't need to let anybody make me so mad that I end up in trouble all the time. Or worse, fail the sixth grade. Besides, I know I can do good work. I can make *100*s on my papers without any trouble, even if nobody else but me cares. I have a good idea for my social studies project too, and I don't want it going to waste. If a person wants to mess up their own life, then go right ahead, but leave me out of it. I don't want to take a chance on ending up some place worse than this. Plus, I don't want to worry Mrs. Cochran anymore than I have to. She's got a nervous streak, being married to a pastor and all. She probably never has been called on to deal with teachers and principals when it comes to her own kids. I just hope Mr. Cochran doesn't blame her for the mess I made and decide to get up a sermon on how to be a better wife.

The next Friday I ask Mr. Franklin if I can stay after again and help him get all his supplies ready for the upcoming week, and he says yes, so I start making that a regular event. Mrs. Franklin always comes to help too. I like being with them, but I don't always know what to say, so I'm glad Ellen is there. When you're five, it doesn't matter as much if you say something dumb.

She starts bringing me pictures from her kindergarten class. I have to say that she colors about as well as she cuts, which is to say not so great, but I always tell her I like them, and she usually gives me one to take home. When I draw a parrot for the tropical rainforest chapter we're studying in science, Ellen tries to draw one too, only hers has color combinations I've never seen on an actual bird. When she's done, she prints E-L-L-E-N across the page in big orange letters that take up nearly the whole sheet.

* * *

Thanksgiving comes and goes at the Cochrans' house. It's mighty quiet, just their family, which is fine with me. A couple of old ladies from the congregation drop by to visit, but that's about it. We have a turkey, as you might expect, and Mr. Cochran watches a football game on TV in the afternoon. I wonder if Daddy is watching one today too. And Mama—what is she doing right now? Is she thinking about Darryl and me?

I spend most of the holiday weekend working on my project, which isn't due till the middle of December, but I don't have anything else to occupy my time.

When school starts back again after the holiday break, I ask Jenna to sit with me at lunchtime. I guess she doesn't mind so much about me not speaking to her the last time because she starts talking right off. It's nice having somebody to smile at for a change. She doesn't say anything about me being in a foster home, so I can't tell if she doesn't know or if she just doesn't care. Either way is fine with me.

Ms. Whitten calls on Tuesday and asks how I'm doing and I say all right. That's really the truth. My stomach feels better, and I'm eating ok and not waking up in the night so much. She says we'll be visiting with Mama right after school on Thursday and then talks to Mrs. Cochran for a minute. I wonder what Mama's going to say this time. She's got to be missing us. We've been gone for six weeks. Maybe Daddy's going with her to those meetings now. Maybe he feels bad about everything now that he's had some time to think about it. Once, when I was about seven, I saw him crying, but he doesn't know I saw. It was when his brother, Uncle Jimmy, got killed in that car wreck outside of Montgomery. So I know he cares about people and misses them when they're gone, which must mean Darryl and me too. Maybe Mama will have good news this time.

* * *

Ms. Whitten is waiting for me outside school on Thursday. She's already got Darryl in the car, and boy, is he happy to see me. He's about to bust with all the stuff he's got to tell about the Burgesses and how much he likes being there. He especially likes that dog of theirs which he says follows him everywhere he goes. He says Mrs. Burgess took all the kids to a movie last weekend, and he ate a candy bar and a whole box of popcorn by himself.

Personally, I don't know why he's so excited about that. People go to movies all the time. Besides, he doesn't need all that junk food.

He's got more good grades to show me too, and he pulls out a bunch of papers. I look at the ones he missed and try to tell him the difference between proper nouns and common nouns, but he's not listening. He just wants to talk about Molly and Catherine Burgess and what all they do, which I don't care about hearing.

We wait in the same room as before at the Department of Human Services. I hate this place. Everything is gray and ugly. If I was one of the social workers, I'd do something to make it a little more cheery. Get me some paint and curtains and some decent furniture for starters.

In a few minutes, Ms. Whitten comes back. Mama is with her and is carrying a big sack that she sets over in the corner.

"Mama!" Darryl yells and jumps up on her.

"My sweet babies," she says, and hugs us both tight. She's not crying as much as last time, which I'm not sure is a good sign. "How are you doing, darlings?" she asks, pulling Darryl down on her lap. I stand in front of her, and she squeezes my hand.

"We're fine," Darryl answers, and starts showing her all his school stuff. She looks at each paper and brags on all of it, especially the math grades. Darryl's so happy he looks like a puppy jumping around wagging its tail. I don't have any schoolwork to show her, but I do have a question or two.

"Mama," I say, "are you and Daddy going to those meetings? Do you know when we're coming home?"

She lays Darryl's papers on the table. "Madelyn," she says, and her eyes look tired when she looks up at me. "I'm trying. I'm going to the parenting classes and I've talked to your Daddy about all this. He knows what he has to do."

"So is he going to do it?" I ask.

79

She doesn't say anything for a long time, just buries her head in Darryl's neck and rocks him. Finally, she chokes something out, but I don't understand, and she has to repeat it. "I don't know," she says. "I don't know."

"Mama," I say, "does Daddy miss us?"

She starts crying hard then, and I don't think she's ever going to stop. Darryl keeps patting her back and telling her everything's ok, but I don't think that's helping. He gives me a mean look too, but I ignore it. There's a box of tissue on the table, and I go get it for her. She blows her nose and wipes her eyes. Then she takes a deep breath and lets it out, but it sounds wobbly.

"I'm not sure what Daddy's going to do," she says finally. "He's been trying to stop drinking, but it seems like it's got such a hold on him. Right after, you know, what happened, he threw out every bottle in the house, and he's been trying, really trying to stop. It about drives him crazy. It's all he can think about every minute, trying to keep from taking that drink."

"If he loved us, he would quit," I say. "All he has to do is just stop. Lots of people quit bad habits. He just doesn't want to."

"Honey, he does want to, but it's not that easy," Mama says. "He goes for a day or two, but he gets to shaking and sweating so bad that he says he just has to have a little something to tide him over. Then it starts all over again."

"I've heard there's alcohol meetings for people who are trying to quit," I say.

Mama nods and picks something off Darryl's shirt. "Yes," she says, "there are."

I wait for her to say something else, but she doesn't.

Darryl looks over her shoulder. "What's in that sack?" he asks.

I want Mama to keep talking, but she doesn't. She just jumps up, smiling and wiping her tears off on her shirtsleeve. "Oh, I almost forgot, sweetie. Those are Christmas presents." She brings the bag to the table and acts all happy. Darryl digs in and lays all the packages out, half for me and half for him. Part of me feels bad for not bringing her anything, but my other side is angry that we have to have Christmas here in this dump.

Darryl tears open his presents and paper flies everywhere. He may be nine years old, but he still likes trucks and anything that makes noise. He gets some racecars, a baseball, and a puzzle, along with a new sweatshirt. Mama pushes her hair behind her ear, and I watch her smile at him with those dimples of hers. She is so soft and pretty, even here in this gray room.

She turns to me. "Aren't you going to open yours, darling?" she asks. I don't feel like it, but I do. There's a blouse, a mystery book, and some other stuff, but I don't really care about them. I say thank you and kiss her, but the only present I really want is to go home.

"What's going to happen, Mama?" I ask, when we've thrown away the bows and paper, and it's time to go.

She doesn't answer at first. "I don't know," she says finally.

"You can move out and get an apartment, and we can come live with you," I tell her. "Or you can make him leave the house, like I told you before. Just till he gets well, Mama. It doesn't have to be forever. Please, Mama, I'm begging you."

"I don't even have a job, Madelyn," she says, buttoning up her coat. "How am I supposed to support all of us? We want to be a family. And besides, your daddy loves you so much." She reaches over and strokes my hair. I want to jerk away, but I stand still.

"Me too?" asks Darryl.

"Of course, you too," she says, and hugs him to her. "Give him a little more time, Madelyn. He's trying, but he needs my help. I can help him beat this. I know I can. He promised he'd quit. He promised. He wants you back so much, and I've got to be there to help him. He sure can't do it without me."

"But he's not going to the parenting classes either, is he?" I ask. "Is he? He's not even doing that, is he?"

She doesn't answer.

"He says he wants us back, but he doesn't do anything to make it happen," I say.

She still doesn't say anything.

"Why do you pick him over us?" I ask. I know that sounds mean, especially after she just gave us presents, but I can't help it.

"Madelyn, I'm not picking him—"

"Yes, you are," I say, "You want him more than you want us, even after what he did to Darryl!" I'm yelling now. "You're a bad mother!"

She takes a step backward, looking like she's just been slapped.

"Is that what you think of me?" she asks. "I'm trying to help your father get over his drinking problem so our family can be together again, and you call that being a bad mother?" She never raises her voice. She just looks at me, and I feel ashamed, but I don't know why. A second ago, I was sure I was right, but maybe I'm not. Maybe she knows what she's doing, and I'm just a dumb kid with no clue about how things work in the grown-up world.

"I'm sorry," I say, looking down. I don't really know if I am or not, but this sounds like what I'm supposed to say.

"I know you didn't mean it," she says, pulling me close and rubbing my back. I let her do it and don't pull away, even though my whole body feels stiff and cold. "I know you're just upset. This is hard on all of us," she says, "but I'm going to help Daddy and then you'll be home. I promise, you'll be home soon." She kisses the top of my head and then puts her hands on my shoulders and makes me look up at her.

"OK now, darling?" she asks, watching my face. "You understand, don't you?"

I nod yes, but I don't think I do. I feel so mixed up inside.

Darryl hugs her again, hard, and then she's gone.

When I get back to the Cochran's house, I take off my coat and get ready for dinner. It's cold and dark outside, but the kitchen is warm and smells like meat loaf. I go to the bathroom to wash up, locking the door behind me. I am brave and strong, I tell myself, like in the collage I made at school. But when I catch sight of my face in the mirror, I don't feel so brave anymore. I'm nothing but a scared little kid with no home of her own. I push hard on my eyelids to try to keep the tears from coming, but I can't do it. A sound comes out of me like an animal would make, like a groan or a howl, and just that fast I grab a towel and push it hard against my mouth. I slide down until I'm sitting on the floor with my back up against the door, and I stay that way for a long time, crying and screaming until I'm all cried out. Then I wash my face, square my shoulders, and go join the family for dinner.

Chapter 8

The next day is Friday, and that afternoon I find myself telling the Franklins everything. I don't know why, but I just can't be brave by myself anymore. Somehow when I start saying it out loud, I end up crying all over again.

At first I feel shy and wish I had just kept my mouth shut, but Mr. Franklin says, "It's all right to cry, Maddie. We all do sometimes. Life can be really hard." That almost makes me start again, but I somehow mange not to.

"Mama doesn't know when we're coming home," I say. "The social worker says Daddy has to stop drinking because it makes him act crazy and mean, but I don't know if he will. Mama says it's hard, but he'd stop if he really loved us, wouldn't he?"

"That's a tough one," says Mr. Franklin. "I don't know if anybody really understands why alcohol affects some people that way, but it does. It takes over their lives, and they're just powerless to walk away from it. It makes them act in ways they never would if they were in their right minds, and no matter how much they want to stop, they can't do it on their own."

"Does that mean he'll never quit?" I ask. I have to know. If I'm never going home, I have to know.

"It's possible to stop," says Mr. Franklin, "but he has to be willing to get help."

"I've heard about those alcohol groups," I say. "Is that what you mean? Because I told Mama about them."

"Yes," says Mr. Franklin, "I'm sure Ms. Whitten has discussed that with both your parents. Those groups have helped a lot of people over the years. Maybe your father will give them a chance."

"Maybe," I say, but it's hard to picture him asking a bunch of strangers for help. I've never heard him say there was anything he couldn't do alone. He crawls under the car and works on it when it's got a rattle, he repairs faucets and toilets when they leak, he fixes anything that's broken. He does it all by himself. And it seems like he's got a tool for everything. But not this, he doesn't have a tool for this. It's broken all apart, and putting it back together is not a one-person job.

* * *

I fall asleep early that night, nearly as soon as Margaret Ann and I get the kitchen cleaned up, but I wake up again about ten o'clock. The house is dark except for some light coming from the den. I wonder who's still up, so I tiptoe softly down the hall. The light is coming from a lamp by the recliner, which means I can't look around the corner without being seen, so I drop down on my knees and wait to see if I hear anything.

I'm about to decide somebody accidentally left a light on when I hear Mr. Cochran talking. I don't hear another voice, so I take a chance and peek to see who he's talking to. His big Bible is in his hands, and he's talking quietly. I wonder if somebody's there that I can't see, so I move really slowly and poke my head around the corner, but he's the only one there, and I realize he's reading.

I listen for a few minutes, trying not to breathe out loud, and I hear some words I recognize from when he was reading aloud at breakfast the other day. Words about how God takes care of us. Words about how God makes the lilies of the field beautiful even though nobody ever sees most of them. Words about not worrying about what tomorrow will bring. I wish I could do that, not worry I mean, but I don't know that God is taking that good a care of me. It doesn't seem like it anyway, so I'd say I definitely have things to worry about. Things like how to make Daddy get some help. Things like whether I'm ever going home. Still, it makes me feel better to hear again about how not even a sparrow falls from the sky without him knowing. Maybe he's watching and I just don't know it.

I back down the hall, stand up slowly, tiptoe back to bed, and crawl under the covers. I try to pray, but I'm too tired, and I don't know where to start anyway. I keep thinking about those sparrows, and I have to wonder: if God knows about them, why doesn't he just reach down and catch them before they hit the ground?

* * *

I hear Mrs. Cochran on the phone on Saturday. When she gets off, she has a funny look on her face and she tells me that the Franklins have invited me to spend the night with them on the last day of school before the Christmas holidays. I don't know why she's so surprised. It's not like I have two heads.

There's a party that Friday afternoon before we get out. Some mothers come up to the classroom and make us play games, then we eat hot dogs and cookies and soft drinks. Jenna is absent, and I don't know what to say to anybody else, so I put some food on my paper plate, take it to my desk, and eat by myself, which makes me feel bad because almost everybody else is in little groups. Sitting alone with no one to talk to is terrible for a few minutes, and I wonder if I'm going to cry, but then the teacher starts reading *A Christmas Carol* out loud. Everybody's supposed to be quiet and listen, so after a while, I quit being so nervous and start to breathe regular again.

I don't mind so much being by myself, but I don't want the Franklins to find out they have some misfit kid on their hands who doesn't have any friends and who nobody likes. I'm afraid Mrs. Abernathy might say something to them since she sees Mr. Franklin at work every day and knows I help him after school on Friday afternoons. I wish they could have seen me at my old school. Everybody liked me there. Angela and I sat together every day. I knew all her secrets, and she knew all of mine. Except for the one secret I never told to anybody. Except for the one that got me here.

Mama always told me that family happenings stayed in the family and that outsiders didn't need to know. She said that no family was perfect, that everyone had their problems, and that we shouldn't air our dirty laundry. I used to think she was right, but I'm not so sure now. Our family might not be all together, but at least Darryl's not getting whipped anymore. I think if Darryl hadn't told, sooner or later Daddy would have killed him. So in this case somebody had to find out. Darryl was braver than I was, and I can say now that I'm proud of him for getting up the nerve to do it.

After school on the way over to the Franklins' house, Ellen tells about her kindergarten party, about playing the games and what all they had to eat. The room mothers brought red punch and cookies, and the kids made gingerbread houses out of graham crackers, icing, and gumdrops. Every kid got to bring home a goodie bag with candy in it too, but Mrs. Franklin says Ellen's will have to go up in a kitchen cabinet and that she can only have one little piece every day. She doesn't want her to get sick from all that junk. Personally, the thought of any more sweets right now makes me want to puke.

We turn in the Franklins' driveway at 4412 Sycamore, which is about a mile from the Cochrans'. I guess I knew teachers had to live somewhere, but it feels peculiar to be walking up the sidewalk and waiting for Mr. Franklin to unlock the door. I try not to stare at everything once we get inside, but I can't help it. There's a fireplace in the living room, a table, a couch, a couple of comfortable-looking chairs, and a picture window across the back wall. In one corner of the room is a Christmas tree covered with all kinds of stuff with a few packages under it.

Ellen grabs my hand and gives me a tour of the whole house, whether I want one or not. The bedrooms are all pretty small. I guess they saved up the extra space for that big room where the fireplace is. She shows me her toys and dolls, and when we're done, we go back where her parents are.

When it's time for dinner, Ellen and I set out plates and silverware and glasses on the table by the fireplace. Mr. Franklin flips on the tree lights and then lights a couple of candles on the table. "To celebrate Madelyn's coming," he says, blowing out the matches. I wonder if he's got me mixed up with somebody else. This isn't my birthday, and I sure can't think of anything special I've done lately. I don't know why he'd make a big deal over me.

When we all sit down, Mr. Franklin reaches for the hands of his wife and daughter, and they in turn reach for mine. I wonder what's going on for a second, but then they all bow their heads to pray.

I'm so shocked at hearing a teacher pray that I can't concentrate much on what he has to say, but it sounds friendly. I guess this is the same God Mr. Cochran talks to, but I could be mistaken. This one sounds like he might be a little closer in, like maybe even in the same room.

It's quiet for a minute when Mr. Franklin finishes, but then we drop hands and start dishing up the food. It's good, but I'm not that hungry after all I ate at the school party. All during dinner the family talks and laughs with each other. They ask me a few questions too, but nothing too personal. Mostly things like what do I like to do and what are my favorite subjects. I say, "art," to the favorite subject question, and they all laugh. Mr. Franklin says, "Good answer. *A*+ for the semester."

After dinner, we all clean up and wash dishes, and then Mrs. Franklin shows me the room where I'm going to sleep. There's a big iron bed with lots of quilts and pillows on it, a desk with a lamp, and a round rug on the floor.

"Do you like it?" Ellen asks, dancing around, and I answer yes. She sure is excited. I don't know if it's because I'm here or if she's always like this with company.

The whole family ends up watching an old timey holiday movie when night comes. The fire is going in the fireplace, and it's so snug and warm. The Christmas tree lights are burning too, red, gold, silver, blue, and green. Ellen sits between Mrs. Franklin and me on the couch, all cuddled up in a quilt her grandmother made, and we drink hot chocolate.

I remember nights like this at home, when Mama made popcorn and hot cocoa, and we all sat together watching television. I would think, now everything is better. I would give Daddy a hug and tell him I loved him, hoping he would remember how it felt to have a nice family that got along and laughed like other families. He would pull Mama close to him on the couch, and she would put her head on his shoulder. They would both be smiling, and I would put my head in Mama's lap, never wanting it to end.

Darryl would be smiling too, wiggling around and trying to settle in, trying to make room for himself on the couch with the rest of us. He couldn't ever get comfortable though, and sooner or later he would end up with his knees or elbows in somebody's stomach. Daddy would look over a couple of times and tell him to stop moving around, but that didn't much help. Then he'd get a little louder and tell Darryl to get still right now or else. Darryl would try, but pretty soon he'd be wiggling again, and Daddy would snap at him, saying, "Are you stupid, boy? Don't you know how to be still? No wonder you get in trouble at school. You don't have sense enough to act right. Is this what you do when your teacher tells you to sit still? You act like you don't have the brains you were born with!"

That's when Mama usually snuggled closer to Daddy and kissed his cheek and reminded him that Darryl was just a kid, that he couldn't help it. Something about her making excuses for him would make Daddy madder and he'd say even a kid ought to be able to do a simple thing like quit moving. By then, nobody would be watching the movie anymore, and there would be cold knots in my stomach. Darryl wouldn't be smiling anymore either. He wanted so bad for Daddy to like him and play with him like the daddies did on those happy TV shows, hugging their children up and telling everybody, "That's my boy, and I'm proud of him." That's all he wanted, Daddy, is that so much?

Instead, Daddy would shrug Mama off and tell Darryl to go get him a beer from the refrigerator. If Darryl didn't do it right that second, Daddy would yell at him. The whole night was ruined then. I'd wait a few minutes, acting like nothing was bothering me, and then I'd get up and yawn and say I was so sleepy I just had to go to bed. I'd try to get Darryl's attention and take him with me, but he didn't always catch on. When he didn't, I'd put my ear up against my door to see if any arguing was starting. Sometimes things settled back down, and everything was all right. But other times, I would hear Mama's voice talking low, too low to hear the exact words, and Daddy talking hard and mean and loud. There would be other sounds then, furniture moving, a yelp from Darryl, and then him screaming and Daddy shouting and cursing. God, God, God, I would put my hands over my ears, not knowing whether I should try to stop it or wait for it to be over. I wanted to go bash Daddy over the head with something, anything, but I never did. I was too scared, sometimes so scared I wet my pants, and me eleven years old.

I'm thinking about it so hard that for a minute I almost forget I'm here with the Franklins. Then Ellen turns, and I snap back to now, here in this peaceful place, and my insides relax. God, I can't go back there, not if it's like that. I won't go back like that.

It couldn't be all that late, but I guess I'm more tired than I thought because I can't even stay awake till the end of the movie. When it's over, Ellen and I go straight to bed. I put on the yellow nightgown I brought and fall asleep as soon as my head hits the pillow.

* * *

Sometime in the night I think I hear a sound coming from the kitchen, but it stops, so I decide I was dreaming. I turn back over and fall asleep again.

* * *

As soon as we all sit down to breakfast, I can tell something is wrong.

"I'm not very hungry," Ellen says. She pushes her oatmeal away and puts her head down on the table.

Mr. Franklin looks concerned. "What's wrong, little one?" he asks, reaching over and putting his hand on her forehead.

"My stomach hurts," Ellen mumbles, not looking up.

"It's all those sweets you ate yesterday," says Mrs. Franklin, clucking her tongue and rubbing the top of Ellen's head. "I'll get something for that tummy, sweetie." She heads toward the kitchen and brings back a pink bottle and a spoon.

"I don't feel good," says Ellen, moaning and holding her belly.

"Do you want me to walk her back to bed?" I ask. I want them to be able to count on me to help during a family crisis.

"Why, yes, Maddie, thank you," says Mrs. Franklin. "I'll be back there as soon as I can put the dishes up and pour her something fizzy to drink."

"I'm on it," says Mr. Franklin, heading to the kitchen. "I've got just the thing."

Ellen gets up and comes with me, her little hand warm in mine, and we walk to her room. When I turn back her bed covers, I get a shock. There are candy wrappers everywhere. All empty.

"Ellen!" I say, "What did you do?"

She just stands in the middle of the floor with her eyes open wide, not saying anything.

I'm panicky for a minute. I have to think fast.

"Quick!" I say finally," get those and put them in the trashcan. Hurry! Hurry!"

"I don't have a trashcan," she says.

"Well, put them in a drawer! Hurry up!"

She doesn't move, so I scoop up the wrappers myself and shove them into her top dresser drawer just in time. Right as I slam it shut, Mr. Franklin appears in the doorway with a cup.

"Hey, hey," he says, grinning. "Just wait till you get a taste of this concoction, straight from the exotic land of Tammaballoo. One sip and your tummy ache is a thing of the past." Ellen giggles. He kisses the top of her head, helps her under the covers, and then sits on the side of the bed

Ellen takes a sip and snuggles down under her blanket. "So how's it taste?" he asks. "Amazing? Incredible? Want a little more?"

"OK," Ellen says and reaches for the straw. Just as she does, she jostles the cup, and it spills all down her front.

"Drink overboard," says Mr. Franklin. "Madelyn, can you go grab me a towel?" By the time I get back from the bathroom, he's peeling off Ellen's wet top. "How about a dry shirt?" he asks, reaching for the dresser drawer. He pulls the drawer open and then turns around slowly with a frown.

"Ellen," he says, looking straight at her for a long minute. "I think we've solved the mystery. Did you eat the candy you had left over from the school party after your mother told you not to?"

Ellen starts to open her mouth, but I beat her to it. "No, Mr. Franklin," I say quickly. "I was eating in here. I'm sorry. I didn't see a trash can, so I just stuck the wrappers in the drawer. I'm sorry. I'll throw them away. Ellen didn't have any. I just got hungry before breakfast this morning. I'm sorry."

Neither of us moves. Out of the corner of my eye, I see Ellen looking back and forth from her father to me, and the next sound I hear is a little sob. Ellen's face crumples, tears rolling down her cheeks.

"No, Daddy," she says, rubbing her wet face on her sleeves, "it was me. I ate the candy, not Madelyn. I'm sorry, Daddy." She crawls out from under the covers and reaches toward Mr. Franklin, but I am faster. I get between the two of them.

My heart is banging against the inside of my chest like rockets going off. All I can think of is Darryl and Daddy. That's not going to happen ever again. Not on my watch. I'm going to stop it here and now.

"Leave her alone," I say. "She didn't do anything. It was me, I swear." I can tell he knows I'm lying, but I have to make him believe me. I have to. He might be nice out in public, but how do I know what he's really like at home?

"Madelyn," he begins, but I cut him off.

"I said I ate the stupid candy! Just leave her alone!" I yell. "Get out of here!" I try to push him back, but he doesn't move. I have to get him away from her. Where is Mrs. Franklin? Why isn't she coming? She's supposed to be protecting her kid.

"What are you going to do to her?" I shout. "I won't let you touch her! I won't!" Before I know what is happening, I am pounding my fists against Mr. Franklin, over and over, screaming and crying with rage, and I can't stop. "Nobody is going to hurt her! Leave her alone! I'll kill you! I'll kill you! I'll kill you!"

Mr. Franklin doesn't move, just stands still and catches my wrists, and after a moment I realize he is talking quietly to me. "Madelyn," he is saying, "Maddie, can you hear me? It's all right, little one. It's all right. No one is going to hurt you here. No one is going to hurt Ellen. Madelyn, I'm here with you. It's ok." He keeps talking, his voice quiet and kind and low, saying the same things over and over, until finally I stop sobbing and gasping for breath. "No one will hurt you," he is saying. "Maddie, shhh, it's all right."

Mrs. Franklin is in the doorway. I don't know how long she's been standing there, but I guess she heard all the commotion. She comes straight to me and holds me close against her, one arm around me, the other stroking my hair. She kisses the top of my head, just like she kisses Ellen. "Oh, dear heart," she says, "I am so sorry about what happened to you and to your brother. I am so so sorry." She sits on the edge of Ellen's bed and pulls me into her lap.

Ellen is crying too, and we all three sit there, one big soggy mess, until Mr. Franklin thinks to grab a box of tissue off the dresser.

It takes a long time for my heart to settle back into my chest and for me to stop gulping air. By the time it does, I feel so exhausted I want to crawl in bed beside Ellen and go to sleep myself. Mrs. Franklin just keeps rubbing my back and rocking me. Mr. Franklin pulls out a chair and sits in front of us, but I don't look at him. Not yet.

"Madelyn," he says, "I'm sure I don't know everything that happened in your family before you came to live with the Cochrans, but I have a pretty good idea. I want you to know that you are safe here, that no one is going to hurt you and that no one will hurt Ellen."

I don't say anything. I am too ashamed. Of course he wouldn't hurt us. I had to know that.

He reaches over and lifts my chin with his finger so that I am looking in his eyes. "Are you hearing me?" he asks.

I nod and then bury my face in Mrs. Franklin' neck.

"You can talk to us anytime, you know," says Mrs. Franklin softly, her cheek against my hair. "We may not be able to change anything, but we're here to listen if you need to talk. Sometimes that helps, sweetheart."

"I'm sorry," I say. My voice is all muffled, but I know they hear what I say because Mr. Franklin says, "It's all right" and gives my shoulder a little squeeze.

"I'm sorry too," says Ellen. "I wish I didn't eat all the candy."

"I wish you didn't too," says Mrs. Franklin, "but I think you'll remember next time. Sometimes a tummy ache can be a pretty good reminder." We stand, and she picks the fizzy drink up again and holds the straw to Ellen's mouth. "Now take a few more sips and then lie down." She pulls a fresh shirt over Ellen's head and tucks the blanket in around her.

"No more candy for a while for you, little one," says Mr. Franklin. He gets up to go, but then stops and turns around. "When you're feeling better, how about you girls joining me in the shop? I've got something to show you."

* * *

Ellen wakes up later feeling better, and she and I bundle up and go out to see what Mr. Franklin is working on. He is covered in specks of mud and sitting in front of a pottery wheel. A chunk of clay sits in the middle of the spinning wheel, and his hands shape it as it turns. We watch quietly for a while.

"It's important to center the clay on the wheel before you begin," Mr. Franklin says finally, nodding to us but keeping his eyes on the wheel. "Otherwise, the whole pot will be wobbly and off balance."

We move closer in and stand beside him, watching his steady hands mold the clay into a short cylinder, then watching him use his thumb and fingers to create an opening and begin to pull the walls of the pot upwards to form a slender neck.

"There are times," he says, working to narrow the pot's opening, "when you see a problem in the clay. Maybe there's an air bubble or a tiny pebble that's gotten in somehow. It's important to correct it as soon as possible so that the bowl or vase will turn out the way it was intended. He pauses, squints at a bumpy place, then smooths it out with his thumb. Weak spots that aren't corrected will make the pot unusable. The important thing in working with clay is to be both gentle and firm. You can't be rough with it or you'll damage it and have to start all over."

He trims the base with a wooden tool and then uses a pointed needle to cut away and even the top. "If I could imagine how this hunk of clay might feel," he says, eyeing his work on the spinning wheel, "I would think it would see this process as pretty painful: being kneaded and pushed and sliced on and pulled. But every move has a purpose. It shapes away or cuts away what shouldn't be there." He stops the wheel, uses a wire to cut the pot free, and then sets it up on a shelf to dry.

Wiping his hands on a rag, he laughs. "Pretty messy job, wouldn't you say?"

Ellen wrinkles her nose. "You have mud all over you."

"I do," says Mr. Franklin, "but it will be all worth it in the end. After this vase dries, after the firing and glazing, it will be beautiful." He laughs again, "I hope."

I think I know what he is trying to tell us, but I have to make sure. After this morning, I know there's a lot I'm mixed up about. I feel shy about asking, but I do it anyway.

"Are you talking just about making pots?" I ask, "or about, well, other stuff too?"

"Other stuff too," answers Mr. Franklin, with a smile. "It's part of my job as a father to help my daughter become who she was meant to be. Yes, she makes mistakes sometimes—so do I— but I think it's important to deal with them the same way I handle this clay, gently and firmly."

He looks at me then. "Madelyn," he says, "I'm not here to judge your parents or what they did, but I do want you to know there's more than one way to handle situations. Raising a child doesn't have to involve hurting him. Or her," he says, smiling at Ellen. "It's a tough job, and as parents, we can reach those places where we lose our tempers and say or do things we never intended, but there are some lines we just should never cross."

"My daddy did that a lot," I say, almost whispering. "He hurt Darryl bad."

"I understand," he says, putting his arms over Ellen's and my shoulders as we walk back to the house. "But you may be a mother yourself some day, and I want you to know that you don't have to do everything your parents did before you. You have your own choices to make."

Chapter 9

It's Christmas Eve, and I haven't heard from Mama again, not that I expected to. Ms. Whitten's probably gone off somewhere for the holidays. I guess even social workers take vacations from all the messes they have to deal with every day. I know I would.

Mrs. Cochran, Margaret Ann, and I spend a lot of time in the kitchen making bread and candy and cookies. I'm good at rolling out the dough and cutting out stars and bells. Mrs. Cochran shows me how to decorate them with icing and colored sugar sprinkles. She even smiles and tells me what a good job I'm doing. Maybe she is strict, but she's got her good points too. I guess you'd have to, to let a string of strange kids move right into your family. We tuck everything down into baskets with new red and green dishcloths on top. I know there are fifteen baskets because I count them. Once they're all filled up, we're taking them around to old people in the church. Mrs. Cochran gives me a name to put on every basket, and I write out tags in my best cursive. I ask her if we can make one for Mama and Daddy and she says yes, that we'll put it in the freezer to keep it fresh until my next visit.

It feels cozy to be inside baking. In just the past week, it's gotten colder than a well digger's feet. I don't much like cold weather. Mama says if I'd put a little meat on my bones, I wouldn't get so chilled, but I'm just not a person who likes to eat a lot.

I remember last Christmas Eve at home being cold and snowy. It doesn't usually snow in Alabama, but it was coming down hard last year, and Darryl was so excited. He kept running to the window and yelling out, "Look at that! It's covering the car! And the trees too! Mama! Come look!" He'd drag Mama over to the window and she'd smile and join him for a minute, then go back to what she was doing in the kitchen. Daddy was quiet and kind of sunk down in his chair, drinking. He never did like Christmas much, but this year I just wanted to tiptoe around him. He'd been laid off in November and hadn't gotten anything else definite yet. He'd had two interviews just this week though, and I was sure somebody would be hiring him soon. I'd been afraid at first that he'd be harder than usual to get along with on account of losing his job, but he just got so quiet over the next few weeks that I didn't know what to expect.

We went to bed early that night, and I made Darryl sleep with me. I'm glad I did, because sometime in the night I heard Daddy yelling at Mama and throwing things around. She was begging him to stop, but it sounded like he was tearing the house apart. There were ripping sounds and something big smashed against the wall, then I heard other stuff breaking.

I pulled the quilt up over Darryl's ears, hoping he wouldn't wake up, and then I locked my door and pushed the dresser up against it. I thought for the thousandth time that I needed to make a plan for getting out of the house in the case of emergency. I knew how to get the screen off my window without tearing it, and I had cleared out a place on the ground outside where we could drop down without crashing into any sticker bushes, but that's where the plan ended. I didn't know where we could go next because I wouldn't know how to explain why we weren't home in bed. I didn't want anybody to think ill of Daddy and accuse him of mistreating his family. Everybody thought he was so fine and upstanding; I wouldn't want people to find out he had this other side to him. Even if it is a sickness, like Mama says, people might not understand. Seems to me a sickness ought to just affect the person who has it, but that's sure not the way it is. This kind takes the whole family with it.

After a while, the house got quiet, and I heard something more terrible than anything that had happened so far. It was the sound of Daddy crying, loud, shaking sobs that scared me and made me cry too. Mama was trying to comfort him, but he just kept crying and crying. Till the day I die, I'll never forget that sound. I moved my dresser back and unlocked my door, ashamed that I had been afraid. Daddy was just hurting and upset, he wasn't mad at us, why couldn't I see that?

That Christmas morning, I made sure I woke up before Darryl did. He was so excited he wanted to run out to see what he got, but I wouldn't let him. I told him to calm down, and we'd go out together. Since he didn't know what went on in the night, he kept trying to jerk away from me, but I held on. Finally, I had to tell him Daddy wasn't feeling good, and he quieted down.

Mama was the only one in the living room when we got there. She was just sitting on the couch in her bathrobe, sipping coffee. The lights on the tree weren't even on. It was just her, sitting there with the curtains closed. I didn't see but two or three packages under the tree, even though yesterday there had been a big pile.

I knew Darryl had been wanting a guitar real bad, and that's the first thing he looked for. Not that he could play it yet, but he figured anybody could be a rock star if they just practiced some. He picked up a couple of gifts and laid them back down, then turned around with a question on his face.

"Mama?" he said.

Mama tried to smile, but it came out all crooked. She reached out and pulled Darryl in close beside her, stroking his hair and holding him. She didn't say anything for a long time, just took a tissue out of her pocket and wiped her eyes.

"Merry Christmas," she said finally. "I love you, babies."

"It's all right, Mama," I said, patting her hand. "It's ok."

"I'm so sorry," said Mama.

"We don't need a thing, Mama," I said, moving in close to her. "We have so many toys now we don't know what to do with them all. The last thing we need is more stuff junking up the house." Darryl caught my eye, but I ignored him. "It's better this way. This is what Christmas is all about anyway, us being together. Isn't that right, Mama? And here we all are. This is just perfect to me. We don't need another thing. It's the very way I'd want it if I could have planned it myself." I took a deep breath, "Now, Darryl, look under that tree and see what you can find. I just bet there's something for you."

Slowly, he picked up the handful of gifts and brought them back to Mama. One had my name on it, and the other two were Darryl's. One of his had been crushed on the side, but it looked like somebody had tried to straighten it out. His presents were a pair of gloves and a coloring book, and I got a pink comb and brush set.

"Ooh, I like those gloves," I said to Darryl. "They'll go good with your blue coat. And they're exactly what you need for playing out in the snow today." I started to fix my hair with my new comb. "I sure needed these, Mama," I said. "My old brush is so worn out it should have been thrown away months ago. Thank you." I gave her the biggest smile I could come up with. "Now, how about we fix us up some breakfast?" I got up, plugged in the tree lights, and pulled Mama to her feet. "Come on, let's get some bacon and biscuits going. Doesn't that sound good, Mama? I know I'm hungry."

I walked Mama to the kitchen and helped her get the pans out. I noticed some busted pieces of plastic under the table when I went to set it, so I got the broom and swept them up. The garbage can under the sink was nearly full, and I started out the door with it.

"Madelyn," Mama said, and then stopped.

"What, Mama?" I asked. "You got anything else you want carried out?"

She didn't answer, just shook her head and turned back to the stove. I opened the door and went on out without even a coat on. The big metal trashcan was under the eave of the house, so it wasn't covered in snow like everything else was. I lifted the lid to toss the bag in and saw it was nearly full already, even though the garbage men just came day before yesterday. What in the world? I thought.

Torn up Christmas wrapping paper was crammed inside. I saw the arm of a purple teddy bear, ripped, with stuffing bulging out, and a green shirt with the tag still on, slashed to shreds, like somebody had taken a knife to it. Underneath the shirt box was a crushed guitar, red and shiny, just like what Darryl wanted. I closed the trashcan lid, went to my knees, and vomited in the snow. I couldn't even move for a few minutes after that, trying to get my stomach to stop rolling. I just stared down at my mess against all those pure white crystals.

"Madelyn?" It's Jackie, holding a warm butter cookie up to me. I have to stand there and look at him for a minute before I remember where I am. "Do you want one, Madelyn?"

"I love the oatmeal raisin ones," Margaret Ann is saying, taking a nibble. She and Mrs. Cochran are tying ribbons around the baskets of goodies, and I realize I have been rearranging baskets on the kitchen counter without even knowing it.

Mrs. Cochran gives me a smile as we finish up, but I don't feel like smiling back. I mumble something, then head down the hall to my room. I wonder what my brother is doing today, and the thought of him makes me so sad I want to cry. I wish I could give him the little guitar he wanted so badly, wish I could put it in his hands and see his eyes light up with joy, wish he could know I love him. Is he somewhere thinking of me too?

* * *

Mrs. Cochran knocks on my door and says it's time to deliver the baskets, but I tell her I don't feel like going, and she doesn't make me. Mr. Cochran is in his study if I need anything, she says.

It's still light outside, so I decide to take a walk through the neighborhood while they're gone. I put on a hat and my warm coat on account of it being so cold. This is a small town, smaller than where Mama and Daddy live, and there are vacant lots and patches of trees right here in walking distance. I get to one of those spots and decide to take a path that somebody must have made before me. The tree branches are bare, and I can see straight up through them to the sky. I climb over a rotten log, pass a big gray rock, and keep going. My boots make crunching noises, and I pick up a dead stick to wave in front of me in case I accidentally run into any spider webs.

In school they told us that Cherokee Indians used to live in this part of Alabama, so maybe I'll find some arrowheads. It's funny to think about other people being here in this exact place so many years ago, gathering food and having families and making all their own clothes. I think I would have liked living back then.

After I walk a ways, I find a place just to sit and be quiet in the cold still air and breathe in and out. That's all I do for the longest time, just take long, deep breaths with my eyes closed. I wonder if my life will always be like this, if I'll always be hurting and alone. The Cochrans talk about God a lot and live together in the same house, but they don't seem too close, it seems to me. I guess having your family around is no guarantee you won't be alone.

The Franklins believe in God too, but it's different. They pray to him like he's a real person and not some scary giant. I used to like the thought of Jesus petting little lambs all around him, but Mr. Cochran about ran that out of me with his church hollering. Now that I'm getting to know the Franklins, I'm thinking that maybe the problem is with the Cochrans and not with God after all. The Cochrans aren't so bad though, not really. They could be a whole lot worse. I just don't think I'd want to be in a pastor's family on a permanent basis, is all. I would not want people watching me all the time, trying to make sure I was always being a good example.

I think the worst part of being a pastor, though, would be if you stopped believing in God. Then you'd be out of a job. So even if you were just mad at God for a little while, you better not tell anybody. I say, if that's what you're planning on being, you better get all that figured out while you're still in pastor school.

As for me, I still get mixed up thinking about God. He doesn't go around making people do the right thing. I know that for sure. If he did, nobody would ever kill anybody else or rob stores or lie. He doesn't keep cars from crashing or people from getting diseases either. The nicest girl I ever knew at my old school drowned in her cousin's swimming pool, and I know nobody, including God, wanted that to happen. He doesn't want parents to leave off taking care of their children either, but lots of parents do. Darryl and I are not the only kids in foster care.

My lucky penny is deep in my coat pocket. I turn it over and over in my hand, wondering what God does and what he doesn't do. I don't know if I'll ever get it figured out.

* * *

It's getting colder and darker, so I follow the path back out of the woods and up the street toward the house. I'm feeling better than I was. Maybe it's the cold air. I stand out in the yard for a few minutes looking through the front windows. I guess Mr. Cochran is still in his study going over his next sermon. Jackie, Margaret Ann, and their mama aren't back yet, so I decide just to sit on the steps and wait for them.

In the light from the window, I can see my breath coming out in clouds. I think about the Indians again and wonder if I could send smoke signals with my breath, like they used to do with fire and blankets. I shoot out a few puffs and then start to laugh at how silly I must look. Through my giggles, I make up whole sentences under the starry sky and watch each word dissolve.

I wonder if God is looking down and figuring I've lost my mind. Here I'm supposed to be celebrating the birth of his son tonight, and I'm out in the back yard imitating Indians. I don't think he's mad, though, I think he's laughing and wondering what in the world he's going to do with his crazy little Madelyn girl.

* * *

The last thing I remember this night is Mr. Cochran reading aloud to the family in his deep voice.

"And it came to pass in those days, that there went out a decree from Caesar Augustus that all the world should be taxed. And all went to be taxed, every one into his own city. And Joseph also went up from Galilee, out of the city of Nazareth, into Judaea, unto the city of David, which is called Bethlehem, to be taxed with Mary his espoused wife, being great with child. And so it was, that, while they were there, the days were accomplished that she should be delivered..."

It seems like only a few minutes later that he is finishing with, "They returned into Galilee, to their own city Nazareth. And the child grew, and waxed strong in spirit, filled with wisdom: and the grace of God was upon him." Mr. Cochran might be a scary preacher, but he sure knows how to read that story and make it sound like the most wonderful thing that ever happened. I can just about see the stars and the shepherds and the baby in Mary's arms. I can imagine the angels spreading their wings and singing in the night. I sneak a look at Jackie, and he looks so relaxed and sleepy, leaning up against his mother. She's rubbing his back through his pajamas. I wish Daddy would have read out loud to Darryl and me sometimes. I wish he would have rubbed Darryl's back like that too.

We go right to bed after that and wake up early in the morning. I take out the presents I made for everybody and carry them to the den with me. I didn't have money to spend, so I did drawings and then added lots of color to make them look more life-like. The one for Mr. and Mrs. Cochran shows them walking into the church. I drew Jackie playing football, and Margaret Ann's shows her holding a kitten in her lap. They turned out pretty good, if I do say so myself. I'm not sure I got the faces just right, but you can definitely tell who they are. I did drawings for the Franklins too, but I'll have to wait until school starts back up again to give them theirs.

There are carols playing on the radio, and Mrs. Cochran serves us all hot apple juice and cinnamon rolls. I feel a little shy at first about having Christmas here, but I get presents along with everybody else. They give me a necklace and a new skirt and a collection of stories about great inventors, which I can't wait to read. I'm happy they don't make too big a deal out of presents. If they did, I might start worrying that what I give them isn't good enough, but everybody seems to like theirs. Mrs. Cochran says she's impressed, that she hadn't known I could draw so well, and Margaret Ann says she's going to put the kitten picture in a frame on her dresser. Even Mr. Cochran says that I have real talent. He says I ought to use it for the Lord, a comment that does not surprise me. I don't know why he can't just say "good job" or "thank you very much" and leave it at that, like regular people.

Even so, it's a good feeling to be together and know they like me and don't mind me being here. The Cochrans aren't exactly the kind of family I would want, but they have their own ways of caring about each other. Personally, I think they have a lot on them, always having to be so perfect all the time. They probably do the best they can.

We go to church after that, shivering and bundled up against the cold. It's all about the birth of Jesus, *Hark the Herald Angels Sing, Joy to the World,* and *O Come All Ye Faithful.* I don't think of Indians even once.

Chapter 10

We get to see Mama just once in January, and it looks to me like nothing has changed. I know married people are supposed to stick by each other through sickness and health, like the Bible says, but who's supposed to stick by the kids? Mama says to be patient and that we shouldn't give up on Daddy, but facts are facts. He's not going to quit drinking, and she can't make him. I get so tired of trying to work it all out in my mind that sometimes I just want to scream.

Things are better at school. Jenna and I sit together at lunch, and sometimes Katie too. I don't tell them much, but some things they already know, because like Mr. Franklin said, this is a small town. I'm not feeling so strange anymore about staying with the Cochrans, but I miss Darryl a lot. I don't understand him. I thought he loved me more than about anybody, but it seems like every time we talk on the phone, he's going on and on about the Burgesses and their kids and that stupid dog. We never have a pet, so he thinks he's died and gone to heaven. Personally, I never have been too crazy about dogs or cats, but if somebody offered me a horse, I wouldn't turn it down.

The biggest thing that happens in January is Ellen's kindergarten program, which is on the third Friday night. The Franklins invite me to go with them. Ellen is so excited I'm afraid she'll wet her pants onstage. She's supposed to be a flower, so she's all dressed up in green tights and a purple leotard. Not a good color combination in my opinion, but that's a flower for you. She's also wearing purple petals made out of crepe paper, attached to a sort of crown that Mr. Franklin made for her. She's lucky she's got an art teacher for a daddy.

The night of the program is bone-chilling cold, and we're all happy to be headed into the school auditorium so we can warm up. We get a good seat, up in the fourth row so Ellen can see us when it's her turn to be on stage. At seven o'clock the lights dim and the curtain rises.

Now, I'm not going to say the program is all that wonderful. I have a lot of experience with school plays, being in the sixth grade now, so I should know. Without even watching I can tell you that there's going to be some talking, some singing, some dancing, and some more talking and singing. Then everybody's going to bow, a couple of teachers will stand up and say let's give them another hand, we'll clap again, and then we're out of here. Believe me, I know the routine. If my career plans fall through, I can always be a director.

I still sit and watch though, because I know Ellen will ask me later to tell her everything I liked about it. It's hard to hear some of the kids, even sitting up so close. A couple of boys can't remember what they're doing up there, so they just stand and stare at the audience, trying to find their moms and dads. When they do, they wave and a few people laugh. The songs are all right though. They're definitely good and loud, mainly loud. I recognize them from Ellen singing them to me on Friday afternoons.

I remember Darryl's school play when he was in second grade. I helped him get ready that night. It was in November and the program was supposed to be about harvest time and being thankful. I don't know how town kids are supposed to know anything about harvesting, as all that is done with tractors out in the country.

Darryl was a pumpkin in his program. Seems to me like they could have done better at assigning parts. He's too skinny for pumpkin status, I told him, but that's what his teacher wanted, so that's what she got. Mama would've sewed his costume maybe, but she was doing a lot of crying around then, so she wasn't much help.

I got two pieces of poster board and some orange paint and drew lines with a black magic marker to make it look like a real pumpkin. It's amazing what you can do with markers. I've done enough drawing to know that. Then I glued the pieces together at the top and cut out a hole for his head. Darryl was sitting there at the table beside me while I made it, and I almost felt like I was his mother and he was my little boy, he was so excited and proud. It fit him just fine.

When it was time to go, we knocked on Mama's door, and she came out after a few minutes and drove us up to the school. At first, I thought she wasn't even going to get out of the car, but I said, "Come on, Mama, let's go watch Darryl. He's been practicing." So we went in and got second row seats.

When the curtain went up, there were hay bales and real cornstalks on the stage. And then the kids started walking out and saying their speeches into the microphone. This tall kid was a cucumber, which turned out not to be so embarrassing because he had such a good costume. His mother must have gone out and rented it or something, although I can't think for the life of me what kind of store would carry cucumber suits. Then there were a couple of apples, a yellow squash, potatoes, and an eggplant.

It was nerve-wracking waiting for Darryl to come out. I glanced up at Mama a couple of times, but her eyes were kind of glazed over, and I don't think she was really seeing anything.

Finally here he came. He looked so small and pathetic that I felt tears behind my eyes. The glue had come unstuck on one side and he was having trouble holding the pumpkin together. Plus, he must have spilled something backstage because there were a couple of big watermarks and some of the marker had run. One of his shoes was untied too. Why didn't I think to check for that before I let go of him? He walked up to the microphone and started to speak his piece, but he couldn't remember all of it. I could see his eyes looking for me, so I hissed out: "Pumpkins need sun, good soil, and room to spread out their vines." He took a deep breath and said, "Pumpkins-spread-out-their-vines." That was good enough. He smiled at me, and I grinned back big so he could see my teeth. Then I nudged Mama with my elbow and she smiled up at him too.

When we got home that night, I gave Darryl a candy bar I had been saving in my sock drawer. He kept asking me did he do good, and I told him he was the best one in the whole program. He was so happy he didn't seem to care that his costume hadn't lasted long enough to become a family heirloom. He just sat on my chenille bedspread and gobbled down that chocolate. I told him I didn't want any, to go ahead and eat it all, but he made me take a piece. That night I let him sleep with me. The excitement of the play must have worn him out because he was asleep in no time. Not me, though. I lay in bed awake for the longest, just listening to him breathe in and out. He made a fine pumpkin.

Tonight I watch Ellen and the other flowers skip across the stage, bowing and waving their arms to these other two kids who are supposed to be the sun and a rain cloud. All the while a teacher is banging away at the piano. I wonder how it is that every elementary school I know of has one teacher who plays piano. I bet before they get hired the principal asks them if they can play, and then he makes sure he picks somebody who does so he won't have to worry about who'll do the programs.

I glance over at Mr. and Mrs. Franklin, and they are so caught up with Ellen's flower act that they don't know anybody else is in the world. I think what I see in their eyes is true love. It doesn't matter to them that Ellen can't draw or read very many words or that she took candy she wasn't supposed to have. It's like they don't see any wrong in her at all.

I wonder how that feels. I wonder what it's like to never worry about whether you'll make good grades or be the prettiest or win an award. You just know your mom and dad will love you anyway. It's bound to feel good, but I don't think that's Daddy's take on things at all. I don't want to chance it with Mama either, seeing as how she doesn't seem to be in any hurry for Darryl and me to get back home.

The show finally ends, and sure enough, a teacher comes onstage and starts in talking. "Thank you all for coming tonight," she says. "Let's give Miss Brannon, our pianist, a big round of applause." We clap and then she says, "And please give our little actors and actresses another big round of applause. They did such a great job tonight." Smile, smile. Clap, clap, clap. "Last but not least, a big thank you to all our parents who worked on the set and the props. You have helped to make this a night to remember. Goodnight, everyone, and drive safely." Clap, clap, clap. And it's over.

Ellen runs down off the stage into her parents' arms, while I stand off to one side just watching them pick her up and hug her. She's giggling and hugging them back, and then she hops down so she can run around with the other kids. The Franklins are chatting with other parents and enjoying all the excitement.

Suddenly I feel like the outsider that I am. Here's this nice little family who all have each other, and I'm this big stupid girl who's always hanging around. I'm not a part of them, even if sometimes I fool myself into thinking it's so. I don't look like them; I don't even know how to act like them. I shove my hands down into my pockets, turn around, and walk slowly through the crowd to the back of the auditorium. I feel tears start stinging my eyes, but I squeeze them back. There's nothing to cry about. I'm not a baby.

I walk outside, but I can't see any stars for all the lights in the parking lot. I don't even try to look. I just sit on the brick wall out front and wait. When they're done gabbing with all the other parents about what a great show it was, they'll come out. I don't care if they do or they don't.

I've heard it said that smoking calms a person's nerves. I myself wouldn't mind having a cigarette right about now. Not that I've ever had one, but if I'm going to start, this would be a good time. I may only be eleven years old, but I have nerves too. I blow frost rings into the night air and pretend they're rings of smoke.

After what seems like a long time, the Franklins come out, hand in hand, and I see them looking around. Then Mr. Franklin goes back inside for a minute and comes out again. I guess they're looking for me, but I just stay sitting where I am. It seems like I can't even move, and not just from freezing to death either. It's like my heart is numb all through.

"Madelyn! Maddie!" Ellen finally sees me in the shadows and comes running. "Madelyn, did you like it? Did you see me in the show?" I nod. She grabs my hand, all out of breath from jumping around, and drags me toward her parents, talking all the way.

Mr. Franklin is wiping his nose with a handkerchief. "What do you say we go for some hot chocolate, girls?" he asks. "I'm in the mood for a celebration."

"Yes, Daddy!" Ellen answers right away, dancing around his legs.

Mrs. Franklin puts her arm around me and gives my shoulder a squeeze. "Where did you disappear to, Madelyn? We lost you in the crowd."

I shrug. "Oh, I just went on out."

We get in the car, and Mr. Franklin turns the heat up so Ellen and I can get warm. All three of them are talking, but I don't pay much attention. I stare out the back window, watching the streetlights go by, and wondering who all lives in these houses close to the school. The Cochrans, of course. We even pass their house. I see a light on in Jackie's room. I wonder if he's in there biting his nails again. I can bet you that sooner or later Mrs. Cochran is going to put a stop to that. I wonder what he'll do then. Probably end up with a tic in his face.

Mr. Franklin turns into a little place called the Dairy Dip, and we take seats in a booth. Mrs. Franklin slides in beside me, and Mr. Franklin orders hot cocoa with marshmallows and whipped cream for everybody. Mine comes, but I don't feel like drinking it. I put my hands around the cup and just hold it, hoping nobody will notice. Not much chance of that, though, with Ellen around. She notices everything I do.

"Madelyn, don't you want your cocoa?" she asks. She's got a spot of whipped cream on her cheek, and she's trying to catch all the marshmallows with a spoon before they melt.

"I don't like chocolate," I tell her. "You can have mine."

"But you liked it at home when Mommy made it," she says.

"Well, I don't like it now!" I know my voice is too loud, but I can't help it.

She jumps a little and then drops her eyes. I don't mean to hurt her feelings, but can't she leave me alone for one minute? I don't have to drink this stuff just because somebody buys it for me. I never told them I wanted any. I hate chocolate. If they want to celebrate, they should order a cake. Maybe even hire somebody to jump out of it and dance a jig.

"Maddie?" This time it's Mrs. Franklin. "What's going on, darling?"

I shrug my shoulders. "Sorry," I say. I'm hoping that covers it, and they'll leave me be. I know I'm being a selfish brat, but I can't quit thinking about Darryl and his pumpkin suit and how all I had to give him was a candy bar. I couldn't take him out for a nice treat. A half-squashed candy bar is a stupid way to celebrate. Mama didn't even try.

Mr. Franklin looks across the table at me with those kind eyes of his. "Maddie, I'm not sure of all the reasons, but I can tell this has been a tough night for you. If you feel comfortable talking about it, you know you can. Whatever you say is all right." He waits quietly for what seems like a long time, but I just can't get the words out.

Last year in school we studied about black holes in space and how not even light can get out of them. How can anybody understand what it's like to have a black hole in your heart that no joy can come out of?

I take a deep breath and manage a smile. "It's ok," I say, "I'm fine." But it isn't, and I don't know if it ever will be.

Out of the corner of my eye I see Mrs. Franklin look up at Mr. Franklin, but all she says is, "We're here for you, sweetheart, if you decide you want to talk."

I go ahead and drink the hot chocolate, just to show them that I'm really all right, but it tastes bitter all the way down.

* * *

The next Friday after school, I'm helping Mrs. Franklin in the art room when I gather up my nerve and ask her a question that's been on my mind for a long time. "Do you ever get mad at God?

I mean really mad, like you can't believe anything he says because nothing is working out the way it's supposed to?" I don't look up from the paint tray I'm washing. "You and Mr. Franklin seem like you think God is always taking care of you. I can tell you for a fact, he doesn't do that for everybody. Like Darryl and me. It seems like he doesn't care what happens to us."

Mrs. Franklin pauses before she answers. "I definitely understand that feeling of being forgotten by God," she says slowly. "I can tell you, Maddie, that I've wrestled with that one many times in my life." She puts the top back on a box of pastels and stares past me out the window for a long moment. "You may think our family has had it easy, but the reality is, nobody has a perfect life. I was fifteen when my mother died of cancer, and I remember I was so angry with God. For a long time, I had nothing good to say to him. I just couldn't understand how he could let it happen, you know. My father moved us across the country a few months after that, and I was so lost. My friends were gone, my mother was gone, and I felt like I had no one to turn to, no one who cared about me." She stops to take a deep breath. "There were other times too, of course, but the worst has to be when Ellen and I were in the car accident, and I lost the baby I was carrying."

"Your baby died?" I ask. I must look shocked because she smiles at me a little, in a sad way.

"I haven't told you about that, have I?" I shake my head. "It was almost two years ago," she continues, "and it was such a very hard time for us. For me especially, I think. I was so angry with God and so hurt. The doctor had said that that was the last baby I'd be able to have, and then even that was taken away. I blamed God, and I guess you could say that for a while I hated him."

"You hated God?" I ask. I had never thought about grownups hating God, much less admitting it to a kid.

She nods, looking out the window again at something far in the distance. "We had a lot of conversations, God and I, mostly my yelling and crying and his listening. There were days, months even, when I could barely take care of Ellen I was so heartbroken and furious. I'd put my boots on and go off in the woods for hours at a time and leave her here with her dad."

"What did you say to him?" I ask. It's hard to picture Mrs. Franklin yelling at anybody, much less God.

She smiles. "Oh, I imagine nothing much different than what other people have said over the centuries."

"You mean lots of people have felt that way?"

"Oh yes," she answers. "Think about wars and poverty and disease and hunger and violence. Think of mothers and fathers all over the world who have lost a child. Think of children who have lost parents or brothers and sisters. There is so much sadness. People turn to God wanting answers and relief. We feel that if he's so powerful, he should stop all the bad things we go through."

"Well, shouldn't he?"

"I'm not so sure. I don't think God is in the business of changing the laws of nature or biology to fit what we want. Oh, maybe sometimes he does, but that's what we call miracles."

"But it seems like some people never have anything bad happen to them."

"I know," she answers. "It does seem that way. I expect if they live long enough, though, even those people will go through something that sets them back on their heels. It's just the way life is."

"Do you still think about the baby a lot?" I ask.

"I will always think about him, probably for the rest of my life. I will remember what would have been my little boy's birthday; I'll imagine what he would have been like starting school, growing up, going off to college. I will always miss him." Tears pool up in her eyes, but she is smiling.

"How did you get over being so mad at God?" I ask. "How did you start liking him again?"

"I'm not sure I can tell you exactly how it happened," she answers. "I know I kept talking, kept yelling, and eventually I found my way. I think I finally realized that some questions don't have answers. Maybe we don't even know the right questions to ask." She smiles again, stacking the clean paint trays on the counter and then reaching into a cabinet for drying rags. "After so much grief, I thought life would never be happy again, but it is, Maddie. It's good."

"Hating God is bad though, isn't it?" I ask.

"Oh, I don't know," she answers. "I expect both love and hate are pretty natural when you've known somebody a long time. I think that hiding what's going on is what traps you and keeps you from getting past the hurt. What's important is that you talk to God about what's happening in your life, both the good and the bad."

"I don't see how talking helps."

"It does, though, if you're honest. You begin to realize deep inside yourself that, whether or not circumstances remain the same, he understands you and loves you. And that matters more than anything else. Then too, good things can come out of even the worst situations."

"Like what?" I ask. "What good could come out of a baby dying?"

"Well," she says, "even though I don't think God brings hard times into our lives, I think he sometimes uses them to teach us things we might not learn so well on our own. Like how to notice when people around us are hurting and how we can help them feel better. The changes that happen in a person's heart are miracles too, you know." She smiles as she hangs the rags up to dry.

"Do you think something good can come out of the bad stuff happening with Mama and Daddy and Darryl and me?" I ask.

Mrs. Franklin looks at me, tears in her eyes again. "Yes, Maddie. Even this, as terrible as it is."

I am quiet then, turning the thought over and over in my mind and staring out the classroom window at the bare and frozen ground.

This God stuff sure is confusing. I thought he would make things better if a person just asked really hard, but I guess he doesn't always do that. For the life of me, I don't know why. And I'll probably never know, if smarter people than me have been trying to understand it all these years and still can't figure it out.

But I do know one thing. I know how it feels when somebody cares about you. I know how it felt on that morning when Mrs. Franklin held me at their house after Ellen ate all the candy. She didn't change anything. All she did was put her arms around me and let me cry. She understood. Maybe that's what God does too. Maybe when the tears come, he just holds you close in his arms.

I can't speak for anybody else, but that sounds pretty good to me. In fact, it sounds like it just might be good enough.

Chapter 11

Ms. Whitten takes Darryl and me to visit with Mama every two or three weeks, but it doesn't seem like much is changing. Seems to me that sooner or later she's going to have to figure out which side of the coin she's on, because there's no balancing it in the middle. She always asks how we're doing and wants to hear about our schools and any new friends we have. I talk some about Margaret Ann and Jackie, but I can tell you for a fact that I hear more about the Burgesses than I care to. Darryl asks about Daddy too from time to time, but I don't want to listen to the same tired old excuses, so I generally try to change the subject. I've figured out by now that there are worse things than being in a foster home.

The Cochrans are nice enough, even if they are a little too stiff and proper for my taste, but mostly I look forward to being with the Franklins. They've gotten into the habit of inviting me over to spend the night about once a month. Mrs. Franklin, Ellen, and I are studying out a little garden we want to plant as soon as it warms up, picking out the seed packets and what should go where. I've never grown food before, so it should be interesting. Mr. Franklin spends most of his time in his workshop behind the house, trying to get ready for an art show in May. He's already made a bunch of vases, some cups, and a whole set of blue speckled plates and saucers. They're not perfect, like the ones in fancy stores, but I hope people will buy them anyway.

This particular Friday night, I read Ellen a couple of storybooks and then work on a science report for school. That takes most of the evening, as I have to make a poster to go along with it. Lucky for me, the Franklins have a lot of good art supplies.

After dinner, we watch a movie and make some popcorn. Ellen wants me to braid her hair, and I do, but it's not that long and I have a hard time getting it to look good. Still, she's satisfied.

"Fix Maddie's now, Mommy," she asks.

"Do you want me to?" Mrs. Franklin asks. I say yes and scoot over on the rug between her knees. Mama used to braid my hair sometimes, and I loved the feeling of her brushing from my scalp all the way to the tip ends. It felt so good. Mrs. Franklin does it now, parting it in the middle, brushing it, making a long braid, and tying it with a ribbon from her sewing basket.

A couple of hours later I'm about down for the count with my head in Mrs. Franklin's lap and Ellen asleep on the other side of her. The show is over and someone has put on some classical music, which will sure enough put me to sleep. It's probably Mr. Franklin. He's always playing that stuff in art class.

They must figure I'm already out because Mrs. Franklin says quietly, "Dennis, what do you think is going to happen to this child?"

Eavesdropping is something I perfected a long time ago. I'm still as I can be and my eyes stay closed, but my ears are wide-awake now.

"I don't know, Pauline. I talked to the Cochrans a couple of days ago. From what I understand, the mom hasn't made any definite decisions about her situation."

I feel Mrs. Franklin's hand smoothing my hair. "She's such a sweet child," she says. "This has been awfully hard on her."

"I know," Mr. Franklin answers. "At least school is going better. Her homeroom teacher says her grades are on track, and she's making some friends." He shifts in his chair, and I hear him poking the fire.

"That's good," says Mrs. Franklin. "Well, we'll just have to wait and see what happens. In the meantime, I'm really enjoying having her around. It's nice for Ellen to have someone to look up to. She loves her like a sister, you know."

Mr. Franklin chuckles softly, and I can imagine the crinkles around his eyes. "Madelyn's a great kid. Strong and spunky."

"Maybe too strong," Mrs. Franklin says. "I think she tries to hold a lot of hurt inside. She pushes it down until she can't stand it anymore, and then she just explodes."

"Pushing it down is probably the only way she's survived so far," Mr. Franklin says. I don't have to see his face to know the smile crinkles are gone. "I remember how rough it was growing up with my own dad. He was always on a drunk. Sometimes I wonder how we made it out alive. I can tell you, that's no way for kids to live." He pauses and I hear the fire popping and snapping. "Still, I think our little Maddie's going to be all right. Not much gets by her."

They are quiet for a long time, and I don't figure I'm about to hear anything else interesting, so I let out a little groan and turn over, my eyes still closed. Mrs. Franklin strokes my hair again. "We'd better get these gals tucked in," she says and helps me to my feet. "Madelyn, time for bed," she says softly, guiding me down the hall. Mr. Franklin follows, with Ellen in his arms.

* * *

Ms. Whitten calls on Tuesday to say that Daddy will be coming to the visit with Mama this next time. I can barely keep my mind on my schoolwork, wondering how it's going to go. I wish she wouldn't even have told us ahead of time.

We haven't seen Daddy since October. What's he going to say? Is he going to tell us he's stopped drinking once and for all? Does this mean we're going home?

* * *

The first Thursday in April Ms. Whitten picks Darryl and me up, and we head to the state office building. The sky's been dark and stormy-looking all day, and the rain's starting to come down now, so Ms. Whitten has to concentrate hard on her driving. Darryl is talking ninety to nothing, as usual, but my stomach is so twisted around that I can't say much of anything.

They come in the room together, Mama and Daddy, holding hands. Her eyes are sparkling, and Daddy is grinning fit to beat the band.

"Daddy!" Darryl shouts. Daddy squats down and Darryl jumps into his arms, hugging and laughing. Daddy squeezes him tight and musses his hair. I guess Darryl's forgotten how it feels to be jerked off his feet and whipped like a dog, but I haven't. I hug Daddy too, but not that hard.

"How's my little buddy?" Daddy asks, sitting down and hoisting Darryl onto his lap. "You being a good boy?"

"Yes sir," says Darryl. "I have a dog now, Daddy. His name is Dean." Darryl keeps on chattering, all excited-like and smiling. Mama's smiling too and unwrapping a plate of cookies she brought for the four of us. She puts them out on the table and Darryl grabs a handful. He's still swinging his legs and chewing, with crumbs all over his mouth, when he says, "Daddy, can we go home with you today?"

I notice Mama get real still. I guess she's wondering what Daddy's going to say, just as much as I am.

Daddy sets Darryl down but doesn't take his eyes off him. He's leaning back in his chair now, smiling and rubbing his chin. "Well, son, now that all depends."

123

"On what, Daddy? What does it depend on?" Darryl asks. "I want to go home with you."

"I want you home too, buddy," Daddy says, "but the judge and that lady's got to agree to it." He jerks his head toward Ms. Whitten who is filling out some papers at the other end of the table. She glances up over her glasses and frowns a little.

"When do you talk to the judge?" I ask.

"Next week," Mama answers.

"And what are you going to tell him?" I ask, looking at Daddy real steady. I have my arms crossed, and I'm standing right in front of him where he can't miss me.

"Well, little girl," Daddy answers. "That's not really any of your business, is it? That's between me and your mama and the court. We're the adults here, and we know what we're doing. Don't you worry about it. If I said you're coming home real soon, then you're coming home real soon."

"Are you going to one of those alcohol groups yet? Are you going to stop drinking?" I ask.

Daddy just stares at me for a minute before he answers, and I stare right back. If it wasn't for Ms. Whitten, I wouldn't have the courage, but I know she won't let anything bad happen here. "Let me tell you something, little Miss High and Mighty," he says finally. "There's not a judge in this country who would begrudge a man a couple of beers after working all day to put food on his table. Not one. So don't you get it in your head that you're going to tell me what I can and can't do."

"So that means you're not going?" I ask. I'm shaking all over by now, but I aim to get some answers and I aim to get them today.

"I don't need permission from you or anybody else to have a beer once in a while," Daddy answers, his eyes narrowing at me.

"And I don't need some damn fool group either. I got a right to relax in my own home. I can handle it."

"No, you can't handle it!" I say. "You can't! You get mean and whip Darryl, and he hasn't done anything to deserve it!"

"If you kids would do what you're supposed to," Daddy says, real sharp-like, "you wouldn't need whippings! My daddy whipped me, and I reckon I turned out all right. You want Darryl to end up being some sissy little panty-waist?"

"I sure don't want him to turn out like you!" I shout.

Mama steps in between us. "Madelyn, what are you thinking, talking to your daddy that way?" I turn to her clenching my fists and hollering: "And I'm not going to be like you, moma! Scared of my own shadow and letting somebody beat up my kids!" I can't stop now. "It's Daddy's fault we're in foster care! It's not our fault! It's his fault and you know it! And it's your fault too, Mama! You let him do it! You knew he was wrong!" I'm shaking harder now, but I don't let it stop me. Somebody's got to tell the truth, and it might as well be me. I got no intention of backing down.

Daddy jumps to his feet. I can tell by the look on his face that he would love to take the belt to me right here and now. He whirls on his heel and goes after Ms. Whitten. "That's what wrong with this country," he snaps at her, smacking his hand down hard on the table. "A man tries to raise his kids right and some meddling social worker snatches them up and makes them think they can say anything they want to and their parents can't lay a hand on them! Damn Communists! You show me a law that says a man can't have a beer in his own home! You show me a law that says a man has to put up with his children back-talking him!"

"Gerald, stop it!" Mama says, "Just stop it! We can work this out! Don't you want the children home? I know you do!"

"I don't have to work nothing out!" Daddy shouts back at her. "Damn sissies! You can go to hell, every one of you!"

"Daddy, please," Darryl begs softly.

"Mr. Bradshaw," says Ms. Whitten, gathering her files, "perhaps it's best if we draw this visit to a close and schedule a meeting for another time."

"I got nothing else to say," says Daddy. "The damn government's going to hell in a handbasket, trying to tell a man how to run his own household! How's a boy going to make it in this world if he's not tough? The whole country's being run by women!" He jerks his jacket up off the table, stomps out, and slams the door behind him. Mama just stands there staring after him.

"I'm not going home with him," I tell her after a long moment. "Not ever. You can do what you want, Mama. Darryl and me are not going home with him."

"But Madelyn..." Darryl starts.

"No," I say firmly. "Not you and not me." My hands are in my pockets, and I feel the hard edges of my lucky penny. "You take your pick, Mama. It's Daddy or us. Darryl and me are going to be all right either way." I don't take my eyes off her.

Mama is looking at me like I'm some stranger she's just met. "Madelyn..." she begins and then stops. She glances over at Ms. Whitten helplessly and then slowly slumps back down into a chair and drops her head into her hands. She doesn't move for a long moment, and I can tell she is crying. I don't say anything though.

"Nothing's going to change, is it?" she finally says, her voice muffled and low. She sounds more beat down than I've ever heard her.

"Sure it is, Mama," says Darryl, coming up behind her and putting his arm around her shoulders. "Daddy will be all right. He's just tired, is all." There is worry in his voice.

Even though her head is down, I can tell that what Darryl says stings Mama like a slap across the face, and she looks up at him with tears streaming down her cheeks. "No. No, baby, no. I won't have you thinking that. No. He's not tired, leastways not any more tired than the rest of us." She looks over at Ms. Whitten now, misery written all over her face. "I can't do anything with him. He won't get any help. In his mind, he's just fine the way he is. What am I going to do? I can't bring you kids home to this." Darryl hands her a tissue and she wipes her eyes.

Ms. Whitten clears her throat then. "Mrs. Bradshaw, children," she says, "let's get together again in two weeks. We all have a lot to think about, and perhaps it's better discussed when emotions have settled down a bit." Mama nods. We leave her to head out into the chilly April rain. I fall asleep to the rhythmic slap of the windshield wipers and don't even rouse when Darryl gets dropped off at the Burgesses.

* * *

Mrs. Cochran looks like she wants to ask me about the visit at dinner that evening, but I got too much on my mind to think what to say.

I lie in bed listening to the rain until everybody is asleep, but I'm too restless to close my eyes for long. I keep hearing Daddy's voice saying, "I reckon I turned out all right." No, you didn't, Daddy, you didn't turn out all right. And if we don't change something now, Darryl will end up just like you. Everything's gone to pieces, Daddy. Our whole family is busted.

Suddenly I sit straight up, remembering the yellow ceramic bird I smashed up against the wall when I first moved in here. I wonder if it's still here. I open the closet and dig around until I feel the shoebox. The pieces are still in it, all right. I lay them out on the dresser, but I can't even begin to figure out what to glue first. They're too splintered up to tell what's what. Just like our family. Too broken to know where to start. I line the empty box with one of my softest shirts and then place each piece carefully back

127

inside. I put another shirt on top and tuck it in so nothing will rattle. Then I put the lid on, tape the whole thing shut, and tie it up in a plastic bag I find in the closet.

Very quietly I put on my coat, fasten it, and slip out of my room with the box. I'm careful to avoid squeaky floorboards as I tiptoe down the hall toward the kitchen. It's dark in there, but I don't have any trouble finding the back door. That will be the easiest one to get out of without anybody hearing. I turn the lock and step outside on to the back steps.

It's cold and rainy, but I don't even think about trying to go back in for an umbrella. I don't have enough hands to carry one anyway. I roll Margaret Ann's old bicycle out of the carport and hop on. Lucky for me, it has a basket on the front, so that's where the shoebox goes. It's dark and there aren't many streetlights, but I know where I'm going. I just wish I'd thought to put on a hat to keep the rain out of my eyes. I don't see any cars out, so I pedal as fast as I can right smack down the middle of the street where there aren't as many puddles.

I whiz past the woods and the vacant lots, then make a wide turn at the corner. There are headlights coming a few blocks away, so I get over to the side and pull the bike off behind some bushes. When the car gets closer, it slows down, like whoever's in it is looking for something. I stay crouched down until it turns down a different street, then I hop back on. My heart is banging against the inside of my chest. I'm scared and soaked to the skin.

I pedal faster and faster, wiping the water out of my eyes as I go so I can read the street signs. I know where I'm going, but it's different at night when the houses are dark. Most of the porch lights are even off. I hear dogs barking from somewhere close, and I speed up, trying to outrun the sound.

Suddenly my tires skid on some loose gravel, the bike slides out from under me, and I land in tall wet grass on the side of the road. My shoe flies off and ends up somewhere I can't see. I look around for it, but it's gone and I'm too scared to be crawling around out here on the ground in the dark. My hands are scraped and hurting, but I pick the bike and the shoebox up and get back on. I only have a few blocks to go and I'll be there. I've got to get to Mr. Franklin. He'll know what to do. He'll know how to put it back together.

I put on one last burst of speed and am breathing hard when I coast into the driveway at 4412 Sycamore. I stash the bike under the carport and ring the doorbell over and over. There's a light on somewhere in the house, but nobody comes right away, so I beat my fists on the door. Rain is pouring off, and I hear dogs barking again. I'm so scared I can't help but cry.

"Mr. Franklin! Mr. Franklin!" I shout. "It's me! Maddie! Hurry! Open the door!" I ring again and again, and finally a porch light goes on. I see Mr. Franklin move a curtain aside to look out. "Please! Open the door! It's Madelyn! Hurry! Hurry!"

Mr. Franklin throws the door open, and I fall inside, a soggy, muddy mess.

"Madelyn! What happened? What are you doing here? Are you all right?" He grabs me by the shoulders. "Maddie, what's wrong?"

My whole body is shaking so bad I can't say anything. All I can do is hold the wet shoebox out to him.

"Dennis?" I hear Mrs. Franklin call, "is that Madelyn?" She comes out of the bedroom wrapping a robe around herself, and I head straight into her arms.

"Madelyn! Baby! What happened?" she asks, holding me tight. "Are the Cochrans with you?" She looks past me to the driveway outside, worry on her face. "Baby, are you alone?"

I nod, sobbing and trembling with relief.

"Come here, baby," she says, sitting down and pulling me onto her lap. She holds me with my head tucked into her shoulder. "Tell me what happened."

"In the shoebox," I choke out. "The little yellow bird. It's broken, and I can't fix it."

I hear Mr. Franklin untying the plastic bag. "Here," he says, "let's go to the table."

I follow them into the living room where Mr. Franklin turns on a couple of lamps and sets the box down.

"First, let's get you out of those wet clothes," Mrs. Franklin says, leading me toward the back of the house. She helps me clean up and get into a pair of warm pajamas with the sleeves and legs rolled up. She towels my hair dry too. In the meantime, Mr. Franklin is building a fire in the fireplace. Even though it's April, it's still cold enough for one.

Mrs. Franklin calls the Cochrans to tell them where I am and that I'm ok. I hear them working out about me spending the night.

Once the fire gets going good, we sit down at the table with Mr. Franklin. He's put a towel under the box, and now he takes off the lid. Carefully, he sets each tiny piece of the broken bird out on the towel, puts on his reading glasses, and examines the lot.

"Can you fix it?" I ask. "I could help you. I know what it's supposed to look like when it's done. Please. Can you try?"

"Maddie," says Mr. Franklin at last, "I just don't think that's possible. It would never be the same."

"But you've got to," I beg. "All the pieces are there. They just have to be put back together. It's a little yellow bird sitting on a branch. See the feathers? And this is part of the beak." Tears are starting to run down my face again, and I can't help it.

Mr. Franklin pulls a lamp in closer, picks up a few pieces again, then slowly shakes his head. "Madelyn, I'm sorry. It just can't be

130

fixed. I'm sure it was beautiful once, but it's simply shattered beyond repair."

Suddenly I am crying hard again, my head in my arms.

Mrs. Franklin rubs my back, and they are quiet for a long time. Finally Mr. Franklin asks, "What happened today, dear? Talk to us."

"My daddy..." I start to say, but I can't finish.

"Did you have a visit today?" Mrs. Franklin asks. I nod, but don't raise my head. "Did your daddy come to the visit?" she continues, and I answer yes.

I sit up straight then, rubbing the tears away, but I can feel my chin still quivering. "We can't go home," I say. "I told Daddy that that we're not coming home. He won't quit drinking and hurting Darryl, and Mama's going to stay with him. So we're not going home. Not ever. She says she can't bring us back into that mess."

"Oh, Maddie," Mrs. Franklin says, pulling me into her arms again. I can feel tears rolling down her cheeks and mixing with mine. "I am so sorry, so very sorry. It must feel like everything is broken." It is quiet then, except for the crackling of the fire and the ticking of the clock on the mantel. She tucks a blanket in around me, and I start to relax against her soft warm body.

"It's ok not to be strong right now, Maddie," she says after a while. "But there will come a time when you realize you're going to make it through this. You'll find your way, I know you will."

We stay like that for a long time, Mrs. Franklin rocking me gently, and Mr. Franklin holding us both.

Chapter 12

I don't wake up until ten-thirty the next morning, and at first, I don't remember where I am, but then it comes back to me. It's Friday morning, and I'm at the Franklins' house instead of at school. My grades are good, so I guess it's ok to miss a day, but it still feels funny. The clothes I was wearing last night are folded up nice and dry on a chair, so I get dressed and go wash my face. Even my shoes are clean and dry.

Mrs. Franklin is cutting recipes out of the newspaper and filing them in a book. She looks up when I walk in.

"Good morning," she says, smiling. "I was beginning to think you were going to sleep all day. Are you hungry, sweetie? Which sounds better to you, breakfast or lunch?"

"Cereal's fine," I say. I pour a bowl and go to the table. The shoebox and broken bird pieces are still out on the towel. Mr. Franklin was right. There is no way it could be put back together. I bet even more parts broke when I had the bike wreck. I don't know why I ever thought it could be fixed. It makes me sad to look at it.

I spend most of the day helping Mrs. Franklin straighten up the house and repot plants. Ellen helps too when she gets home. When we pick Mr. Franklin up in the afternoon, he has a little bag full of brushes and paints with him.

"What are you going to do with those?" Ellen wants to know. Mr. Franklin's eyes are twinkling. "Wait and see," he says.

At their house, he sits down at the kitchen table, turns on the lamp, and motions me to the chair across from him. He puts on his reading glasses and examines a few of the broken bits in the light. Ellen kneels on a chair to watch.

"What do you think about putting all these parts back together?" he asks.

"But you said—" I begin.

"Reconstructing the original form isn't possible, of course. But the pieces..." He pauses, looking at me over his glasses, "the pieces could be used to create a new design. It will take some time and some work, but it might even be better than it was before. What do you think?"

"A design?" I ask. "Like a mosaic?"

He nods.

"I did a construction paper mosaic of a unicorn once," I tell him. I start to get excited now, thinking of how it could turn out.

"You'll need to break some of these even smaller," he says, sorting through the large pieces. He goes to the kitchen and scrounges around in a drawer. "We've got a tack hammer around here somewhere..." He pulls one out and hands it to me. "Keep it all on the towel so nothing gets lost. You don't have to tap hard. Just a little—like this. And don't worry about the table. As you can see, it's been the site of a lot of art projects over the years."

He opens the bag he brought from school and sets the paints and brushes out. "When you're done, give everything a few coats of paint, and we'll go from there." He heads out back to his shop.

I bend over the work and tap, tap, tap until most of the pieces are about the same size. I leave some long and thin, in case I need skinny parts. Ellen watches. I have to give her credit; she's as still as can be and doesn't mess my concentration up at all.

After that, Mrs. Franklin helps me cover the table with newspapers, and I shake up the jars of paint. The colors are shiny and sparkly like fingernail polish. As I finish each chip I place it carefully on a plastic platter to dry. Then I give each one a second coat, just to be sure.

The little pieces look like jewels when I'm finished: tiny blue, green, orange, purple, black, and red jewels.

By the time that much is done, Mr. Franklin is back inside, and we clear the table for dinner. After supper I have to go back to the Cochrans, but Mrs. Franklin says she'll keep everything in a safe place until the next time I come over.

All week I arrange and rearrange the pieces in my mind, figuring where the different colors should go. I'm thinking I'll make another unicorn or maybe a different kind of magical horse. I get it all worked out just like I want it, then decide it's not quite right, and I start all over. It's three weeks before I get a chance to work on it again, and I'm still turning over designs in my mind.

When we get to their house, Mrs. Franklin sets up a card table for me by the picture window so I can leave the supplies out. Mr. Franklin helps me find a piece of smooth wood about a foot square. He says we'll need something to put the mosaic on, and he tells me to pick out a good color for the background. I decide on yellow. Ellen and I take the wood outside, and I paint it bright and beautiful like the sun. We have to wait a little while and then paint it again. When that coat is dry, I take it back inside to the table.

Mr. Franklin says I can make anything I want, so the next morning the real work begins. I take each shiny colored piece and arrange it carefully on the wood, but I don't glue it yet. I want to be sure everything fits first, and it's a good thing too, because it turns out the unicorn doesn't look right with all those colors. I don't like the other horse either. A fish might be ok, but I'm not really interested in fish. I look around, trying to get ideas. A tree maybe? A basket of fruit? None of that sounds like what I really want.

Mr. Franklin sits down at the card table. "Are you making progress, Maddie girl?"

"Not really," I answer. "I thought I had a good design, but everything looks wrong. What do you think I should make?"

"Well, let's see," says Mr. Franklin. "You have some fine colors here. They look almost tropical." He pushes a few blue pieces around on the yellow background and then drops a black chip almost in the middle. It looks like the eye of the bird I smashed.

"Wait!" I say. "Wait! I know what to do! It *can* be a bird again, but different. Is that good?"

Mr. Franklin takes another look at the chips and then smiles at me. "I think that sounds exactly right."

Carefully I pick up each colored piece and arrange it on the board. I am so excited that I hardly notice when he squeezes my shoulder and goes out to his workshop.

The head will be mostly red, I decide, with orange in a few places. And I'll make the body blue and purple and green. How should I do the wings? I work for about an hour before Mr. Franklin comes back inside.

"How's it coming?" he asks, pulling a chair up to the table and picking up a couple of stray chips.

"Good, I think. But I can't get some of the pieces in right. No matter which way I turn them, they still stick out funny."

He laughs, but I know he understands. "You know that's ok, don't you?" he says. "Not everything has to be perfect. In fact, some of those very pieces are what make the design interesting and uniquely yours."

"Yes," I say, but until that moment, I guess I didn't really know it at all.

It's easy when I think of it that way. Mr. Franklin heads on back to his workshop, and I get busy putting a little dot of clear glue on each tiny chip and then placing it back in its spot. The parts that don't fit just stick out, and I decide they are all right the way they are. Slowly the mosaic takes shape: first the head, then the beak, and then the body with outstretched wings. A bright jeweled bird flying against a dazzling yellow sky. The broken pieces are whole and beautiful again. When it's all done, Mrs. Franklin shows me how to brush varnish over the whole thing, and then I put it back on the table to dry. She and Ellen help me clean up the mess and put all the supplies away.

Just as we're finishing up, Mr. Franklin walks in from the shop wiping his hands on an old paint rag.

"Daddy!" Ellen shouts, running to him and jumping into his arms. He lifts her up above his head, kisses her, and then swings her, giggling, back to the floor. It's a routine I've seen a hundred times, but I still can't help but watch.

"Hello, ladies," he says, "how's the project coming?" He leans over to kiss Mrs. Franklin.

"Just fine," she answers, returning his kiss. "I must say Maddie's been awfully busy." She smiles at me.

I glance over to where the rays of the late afternoon sun are shining in through the back window. My picture is drying there on the table. Mr. Franklin follows my gaze and walks over to see it up close. For a long minute, he doesn't say anything, just stands looking down at it. I go over and stand beside him.

"The broken bird pieces," I say. "They're not broken anymore."

He doesn't say a word, just puts his arm around my shoulder and holds me close against his side. I put my arm around him too. The afternoon sun catches the colors in the bird's wings and makes them sparkle.

"It's beautiful," he says quietly. "Beautiful. *Hope is the thing with feathers that perches in the soul.* That's a line by Emily Dickinson I've always liked." When I look up, there are tears in his eyes.

* * *

After that day, I know I will be all right. Mama may have decided to leave Darryl and me in foster care, but that's not the end of the world. Maybe life won't be exactly the way it used to be, but it can still be good.

It's two weeks later when we see Mama again. She comes in alone this time. I know Darryl is nervous, thinking about what happened on the last visit, so he doesn't even ask about Daddy.

Mama doesn't say much at first, just gives us each a hug and sits down across from us at the table. Darryl is babbling on about school, showing her his papers and a good note from his teacher. Ms. Whitten, as usual, is over in the corner with her paperwork. Finally Mama clears her throat and says something I thought I'd never hear her say.

"Madelyn," she begins. "And you too, Darryl. I have to tell you something. I... need to say something to you."

"What is it, Mama?" Darryl asks.

"Madelyn," she says, leaning forward on her elbows and pressing her fingers against her eyelids, "you were right. You were right and I was wrong. Over all these months, I've missed you so much. You have to know that. I thought Daddy would get some help once he realized what he was doing. But seeing him last time with you all..." Her voice trails off.

"I just didn't want to believe what was happening," she goes on. "It seemed like some terrible nightmare. The police coming, you all getting taken away. I thought surely Daddy would realize that if something didn't change, we would lose our babies. I thought I could help him. If he knew how loyal I was, that I would love him no matter what, I thought he would want to change."

She pauses, choking back tears. "I know now how wrong I was to let it go on for so long. I should have done something. We've been talking about these kinds of things in the parenting classes, and after last time, well, I realized I should have put a stop to it a long time ago."

Before, I probably would've patted her arm and told her it was all right, that I understood. But now I just sit waiting for her to finish. I want her to say it. I want to hear it out loud.

"When I saw him with you up here, I knew I was just fooling myself. I saw how things were. Whether he can't change or he won't, I don't know. But I know I want you back home. I want you and Darryl with me. I don't want to live without you." She takes a deep, shuddering breath and continues. "I've done a lot of thinking since that day. A lot of thinking about what I would need to do to make that happen. It's not going to be Daddy and me working toward this. It's just me. I'm scared to death, to tell you the truth. And I know it won't be easy, but we have to start somewhere. I found a little apartment near your old school, signed a lease, and have already moved a few things. I'm going to finish packing and taking boxes over this weekend. I've been filling out job applications too, and day before yesterday I was offered a secretarial position at a real estate office. I accepted it, and I start on Monday."

"You're leaving Daddy?" Darryl asks.

"Yes," says Mama, "It's what I have to do. I've made up my mind." She looks at me across the table. Her eyes are red and sad, but her chin is set. In fact, I can see just a little hint of a smile on her mouth.

"I'm proud of you, Mama," I say. I walk around the table and put my arms around her.

"You're strong, Madelyn," she says, squeezing my hand, "so much stronger than I am. You could see what was going on, and you stood up to Daddy. You told the truth, Madelyn, even when nobody wanted to hear it. And you too Darryl. You are both so brave."

"So we're going home to live with you?" Darryl wants to know.

Mama nods. "I don't know how long it will take for me to get in to see the judge again, but I can tell you for sure you're coming home. When all the details are finalized, Daddy will be paying child support, and that will help. It will be hard, but we're going to be all right. You kids and I, we're going to be ok."

I look over at Ms. Whitten. She is smiling.

Afterword

Mama was true to her word. By the end of June, we were living with her in her new apartment. And a year later, we are still doing fine. She was right about it being hard, as far as the money was concerned, but we didn't mind. We were together and we were safe, and that's more important than having a houseful of clothes and toys.

For the first month or so after moving back in with Mama, Darryl pitched a fit about getting a dog like the one he had at the Burgesses, but Mama said no, we didn't have room for one in our apartment. He wouldn't hush up about it though, so for his birthday, she got him a couple of goldfish. That wasn't exactly the same, but it satisfied him.

As for the Franklins, they still invite me over to their house some weekends. Mama's met them and likes them a lot, so she doesn't mind me going. Darryl comes with me sometimes too. Because of them, I know what a family is supposed to look like and how a father should act. That's definitely one great thing that came out of a long and scary year. And there's another thing too, maybe even more important: in spite of what all happened, or maybe because of it, I know I'm strong. Strong enough to make beautiful things out of what's broken. That's a lesson I'm going to keep in my heart for a long time.

And the Cochrans? Well, I was sorrier than I thought I would be to say goodbye to them. I can't say as I've missed hearing Mr. Cochran holler every Sunday, but they turned out to be all right. I never thought I'd say it, but I kind of miss the Bible reading at breakfast every morning. There were some good parts in there that I didn't even know about before. I learned a few other things too, like how to make Christmas cookies and how a person should not tear up her room when she gets mad. Margaret Ann and Jackie were nice too. I'm glad I got to know them. I hope Jackie's not still biting his nails. It may take dipping his fingers in pepper sauce, but his mama's going to find a way to break that habit of his sooner or later.

I'll never forget the day I left the Cochrans' house. I was all packed up and sitting on the edge of the bed, looking around and waiting for Ms. Whitten to come. My bedroom walls had been repainted a few months earlier, and the busted furniture repaired or replaced. There was a new mirror over the dresser too and pretty new things sitting out to look at: a comb and brush set, a pot of silk flowers, and a little trinket box. A new girl would probably be taking my place before long. I wondered what she would be like and what kind of family she would be leaving behind.

I heard the doorbell ring and voices in the living room, so I picked up my brown suitcase and headed down the hall. Margaret Ann, Jackie, Mrs. Cochran, and Mr. Cochran were all standing there with Ms. Whitten and Darryl. Everyone hugged and said their goodbyes. It felt funny knowing that I'd probably never see them again.

We were all settled in the car, waving and about to pull out, when I told Ms. Whitten to stop, wait a minute. I dug in my suitcase, grabbed something out, and ran past the Cochrans back into the house. I heard Mrs. Cochran ask if I had forgotten anything, but I didn't take time to answer.

I entered my room one last time and walked over to the dresser. Right beside the silk flowers I propped a square of bright yellow sky, a present for the girl who would come after me. *Hope is the thing with feathers.*

Then I closed the door softly and stepped out into the brilliance of a summer afternoon.

LaVergne, TN USA
24 November 2010
206098LV00002B/19/P

9 781451 275391